Piper at the Gates

Piper at the Gates

a novel

Kristina Montesano

Full Court Press
Englewood Cliffs, New Jersey

First Edition

Copyright © 2012 by Kristina Montesano

Published in the United States of America
by Full Court Press, 601 Palisade Avenue
Englewood Cliffs, NJ 07632
www.fullcourtpressnj.com

ISBN 978-0-9837411-8-3
Library of Congress Control No. 2011946207

*Book Design by Barry Sheinkopf
for Bookshapers (www.bookshapers.com)
Colophon by Liz Sedlack*

To: Mom; Dad; Lucky; Jake
CC: Professor Schulman; "ENL 371 Classmates at the College of Staten Island: Spring 2009"; Matt Turvey; Anne Sölter; Laura D'Anna; Justin Dean; Lee Papa; "SEEK"
BCC: Randy Orton; Dante Alighieri; Pink Floyd; Chuck Palahniuk
SUBJECT: Thank You

This novel is for Mom and Dad, who don't read books but who promised that they would read this one. (We'll see.) It's for Lucky, who started this journey with me by resting her head on my leg as I wrote, and for Jake, who finished it by resting his head on my leg as I clicked 'save' and exhaled.

But it's for you, too, for many different reasons—for whoever picks up this labor or love, and heartache, and takes something away from it (not just by stealing it).

With love,
Kris[tina]

1

Good Friday

PIPER, WHAT IS THIS?" My boss, Jan, waved a sheet of bright white computer paper. It had Times New Roman in twelve-point-font, from top to bottom, in what appeared to be one-inch margins. She obscured my view of the Eucharistic cups I was polishing for the upcoming evening mass.

After setting the chalice aside, I plucked the paper out of her hand. I brought it up to my eye line, in order to obscure the view of her lipsticked mouth, in the shade, *Fire Reef.*

Shit, I thought, suppressing a cringe.

"Well?" She moved her hands to her too-wide hips. The knit fabric of her sweater vest was stretching to its limit.

"It seems to be a piece of paper. Computer paper."

Jan rolled her eyes dramatically, exhaling onion breath in the process. She was the monsignor's right-hand woman; cougar-aged, unmarried, with fried blonde hair, and shades of lipstick that burn retinas. Jan's main gripe in life was how she was unmarried, but, as she explains constantly, there hasn't been a man strong enough to hold her down. Whatever it meant, it conjured up gross and unsettling images in my mind. My personal belief was that Jan was the Antichrist in disguise, and she existed only to keep tabs on the Freedom Island Catholics.

"Piper Marino," she sneered. The images in my mind dissipated. "English three-oh-one, Professor—"

"All right," I confessed. "It's *my* paper. *My* bad."

"Your paper, that you printed out here, at work, instead of at your own home?"

"Yes." I lowered my head.

"Using St. Isadore's paper, and St. Isadore's ink, on St. Isadore's time?"

"Uh-huh."

"Let's go talk to Monsignor Lucas."

"Oh, come on," I pleaded. "Please, Jan. Just give me a break, and I promise I won't do it again. I ran out of paper at home, all right? It's only four pages. I brought my own stapler."

"Oh, you brought your own stapler!" Jan hissed. Her attempt to whisper loudly was unsuccessful.

I wasn't going to win the argument against St. Isadore's biggest fan, so I caved in and funeral-marched into Father Lucas's office. It was dressed in mahogany furniture, with a wall-to-wall bookshelf. The priest was sitting behind his desk, his face buried in a novel. When he saw us, the priest waved his hand toward the chairs.

"Please," he smiled. "Have a seat."

Jan jumped in the chair to the right, and I slinked down into the other.

"Father, I'm sorry to bother you like this, but there's a problem. Piper's been stealing from the church."

"Whoa!" I gave the international sign for time out. "Whoa, okay. Hold on. No. I just printed a paper for school."

"That's stealing!" Jan squealed.

"Okay, Jesus—crap, sorry—oh, no." I panicked, fumbling into my pocket in order to retrieve the two singles I had crammed in there for the vending machine. "Here." I stretched my arm out toward the priest. "Please, sorry. Here... this is for the paper. And the ink. The staple's mine."

My cheeks had to be sixteen shades of red. Father Lucas appeared slightly alarmed, but was doing a pretty decent job of masking it. Jan's eyes were popping out of her fat, moose head.

"I want her *gone*," she demanded. "This isn't the first offense."

"What are you talking about?" I snapped.

Jan, smiling like a possum, was utterly delighted to knock me down. "Piper disappears for half an hour each day, and she doesn't clock out or back in."

"Not true!" I glanced from Jan to the priest. "It's fifteen minutes, maximum, and it's to walk my kid sister home. I cut my other break in half so I can take care of it. The only offense is forgetting to clock out and in. That's it." I had won the argument, I was certain. How could I lose when I pulled out the big guns?

"She blasphemes, you know," Jan declared. Apparently, she had a back-up plan.

I buried my face in my hands, and was partially covered by my curtain of blonde hair.

"Piper." The priest leaned forward to pick up my attention. "I've received a few complaints…"

"But, Father Lucas," I protested. I picked my head back up and stared him in the eye. "I need this job. I desperately do. You know that. We talked about it. It's Good Friday. What would Jesus do?"

"See how she makes a joke of the Lord?" Jan shot me a smug look, but I brushed it off.

Father Lucas slowly shook his head and met my eyes. "I'm sorry, Piper," he said. "We have to let you go."

"Please don't," I begged. "I'll watch my language. I don't even realize it."

"I wish it hadn't come to this." He wasn't backing down.

"I wish it hadn't come to this, either." I stood up and smoothed out my pale blue, button-down shirt. "This goes against the principles of our faith, by the way. Maybe I should jump ship to somewhere else, where humanity is key."

"Blasphemer," Jan snarled. "Child of the Devil."

"Janine!" Monsignor Lucas banged his fist on his desk. His framed photograph of Pope Benedict, fell, face forward, onto the floor.

"You know, Jan," I sneered, "If we weren't in the company of a priest, I would tell you exactly how I feel about you."

"Piper—" Father Lucas tried to talk, but I left. I couldn't bear it.

I slid my homework assignment into my bag, and exited the church with an overwhelming sense of despair. I departed the corner and walked down the hill, toward my house. I sat in the backyard, on the tire swing, and sobbed. I turned my head upward to watch the sky. The cerulean blue slid into monochrome as minutes ticked away. The clouds were heavy, pregnant with condensed water. My old religion teacher, Mrs. Hennessey, used to say how it rains every Good Friday because the Lord is sad about the death of His son. It sometimes caused me to wonder why it didn't downpour every day. But after getting canned on not-so-Good-Friday, I totally get it now.

MRS. HENNESSY HAD ALWAYS gotten very annoyed when I tried to argue the April showers logic.

"Maybe the whole tears-of-God thing is just a coincidence," I had once boldly stated.

Instead of entertaining the thought in my eight-year-old mind, Mrs. Hennessey'd been quick to shoot me down.

"You are wrong, you perverse child!"

She had sucked on her dentures, and picked at the imaginary lint on her cardigan. She had them in each shade of gray. Ash. Iron. Lead. Slate. Smoke. Stone. I had been convinced that she kept her old, knobby hands, occupied, so she wouldn't hit us. It wasn't legal anymore.

"Piper Marino," she had rattled. Her accent delved deep into Irish whenever she enunciated vowels. "Romans, chapter one, verse seventeen, says, *For therein is the righteousness of God revealed from faith to faith: as it is written, the just shall live by faith.* Do you understand?"

"Umm... no."

"Do you know what faith is?"

Her weathered, shar-pei face had inched closer to mine. The smell of mothballs had only been faintly masked by Chanel No. 5. I didn't know which one was worse. She'd been maybe eighty years old, and her chalky bones left her gnarled body contorted into a question mark. Because of that, we were almost at eye level.

"Faith? Umm. I dunno. I guess. Maybe."

"It's believing but not seeing. Do you understand now?"

"Like aliens?"

"No. Not like aliens. Like Jesus."

"*Well*," I'd sung. "How about Santa Claus? The Easter Bunny? Tooth Fairy? Umm... Buddha? Can I have faith in Buddha?"

"No!"

"So, um, hang on, Mrs. Hennessey. I can have faith, right? But... I can only, um, have faith... in Jesus?"

"Yes!"

Mrs. Hennessey, fury rising in her cloudy blue eyes, had violently shaken her clenched fists, and abruptly whirled on her heel and hobbled away. Perhaps she just wanted to get away from me. Or, maybe, she didn't know how to explain about faith.

It went on for years, until I'd been Confirmed at the age of thirteen, and didn't have to suffer through her classes anymore. I didn't know who'd been happier about it. Years later, according to my Grandma Flannery who witnessed it, Mrs. Hennessey had been slammed by a delivery truck when she was crossing a busy intersection. She was ninety-five years old when it happened. She didn't die, though. Instead, she'd broken both hips, but those later got replaced with the artificial kind. The truck had actually hit her in such a way that her back was straightened out a bit. Mrs. Hennessey wasn't a question mark anymore. In fact, her body had morphed into what my grandmother described as a parenthesis. I'd guessed it was better.

With the settlement money she had received from Diablo Cola Company, the ancient religion teacher called it quits, and had a mansion built for herself down in Boca Raton. The decision was much to the dismay of my Grandma Flannery, who was anti-Semitic and allergic to oranges. She'd also been appalled that an Irish woman wouldn't want die in Ireland. It took them a few years to build her house, so Mrs. Hennessey had continued living in Freedom Island, across the street from Grandma.

The night before she was to fly down to her new home, Mrs. Hennessey had a massive stroke. It led me to think about how I never spoke to her after I was Confirmed, even though she was Grandma's neighbor. She'd clung to life, even though her whole left side was paralyzed. Her body reformed into the odd shape it once was, and the blue dandelion puff, formerly her hair, was gone. Her hands only got worse, clunky and road-mapped with raised, blue veins, along gigantic knuckles, and crooked, bloated fingers.

And a few years after the stroke, blind, and deaf, and clutching rosary beads on her death bed, Mrs. Hennessey had gone to the great beyond, or wherever, to see if Jesus and Buddha could co-exist in harmony.

Her house, as was written in her will, had been left to St. Isadore's. It sold for a hell of a lot of money. Because of dead Mrs. Hennessey's fortune, there was a massive fountain placed on the church lawn, new stained glass windows put up, a gigantic marble crucifix erected, and a grand piano to accompany the new sound system and instruments. At the back of the church, in a small pewter frame, they'd placed a picture of old Gladys herself, with her pitcher's mitt hands clasped together in prayer. All of her heartache and all she had gotten was a crummy, framed picture, outside of the crying room.

WHEN THE SUN WAS completely gone, I showered my tears away, and relocated to my bedroom; though, I was drawn to the sky, once more. I couldn't, but I knew that I should move away from the puce curtains, and let them fall back into place. They covered the glass doors which made way to the small balcony. It was more like a ledge with a gate, but it was my own. My older brother decided to make the basement his home, and my kid sister was prone to night terrors, so she slept wedged in between my parents. Abigail was sort of an insurance policy, protecting all of us from another unexpected pregnancy. It was just about the only thing that I liked about her.

I trudged downstairs in my Friday night best: an old pair of gray sweatpants, and a deep purple "Dean's List Recipient" t-shirt. It should have read, "I got a 4.0 GPA and all I got was this lousy shirt." But colleges have no sense of humor, except when it comes to spelling and pronouncing last names incorrectly. The professors who weren't Italian-American became surname butchers. Marino became Maniro. Marine. Morano. And, stranger still, "Mario" from a ditzy WASP during roll call.

My sister was the only one occupying the living room. She was on her Easter recess, so I didn't have to pick her up from the bus stop. Cheap plastic eggs in all the Crayola colors were scattered over the dense blue carpet.

"You're a pedophile cupcake." I wrinkled my nose at her.

"Huh?"

"Never mind. Isn't that what you're gonna wear on Sunday? Mom's allowing you to test-drive it tonight? You'll get egg dye and shit all over it."

I stared at my eight-year-old sister, who was wrapped

in yards and yards of bubblegum pink organza. She was standing up. I figured that she was probably afraid to flatten out the bejeweled ruffles, stiffly forming an umbrella shape around her hips, ending just above her knee. On the back of the explosion of cotton candy, there was a ladder of cubic zirconium buttons. They led to a gigantic, lilac bow right on her tailbone. As usual, she was preoccupied with the television, and couldn't be bothered paying me any mind.

"Abigail." I poked her in the ribs. "Are you even listening to me?"

She swerved her head toward me, and I cringed at her glitter-glossed lips. I recognized the shade, *Scallop*, from my mother's collection of *Sea Goddess* cosmetics.

"*What*?" She shifted her weight from one leg to the other.

"Do you know what objectification means?"

"No."

"Well it means, like, to make someone an object. Do you know what I mean?"

"No." Abigail whipped a thick blonde curl off of her shoulder and rolled her navy eyes. She pursed her lips, and one of her thin, light brown brows darted up. Abby was a miniature version of me, only cuter and meaner.

"Don't give me that," I warned. My arms folded across my chest. "I invented it. It's mine. You can't have it."

"I do it better than you," she retorted. "'Cause I have better hair. Yours is all, like, thin. And it's choppy, like uneven grass. Plus, your eyebrow can't jump up *as* high as mine can, because I practice in front of Mom's vanity mirror. And you need to get 'em waxed, by the way."

"Wow. Brutal. Are you sure you're not just some bitchy queen trapped in a little girl's body?"

"Huh?"

"Never mind. Where's Dippy?"

Dippy was what I called my older brother Denny, because he had a tendency to do incredibly stupid things.

"Downstairs, I guess. Can you, like, stop asking me questions?" Abigail whined. "And, like, go away?"

"Yeah. Yes. Hey, listen... I love you, Abby. Okay?"

"I'm gonna yell for Mom in a minute!"

I walked away, wondering how so much had gone wrong in such a short span of time.

DIPPY WAS IN THE basement, fast asleep, and sprawled out on a dense mattress with a memory foam pad thrown over it. He was in Christmas boxers, despite Easter being two days away. The room was a disaster. Dirty dishes were scattered on the floor, and unidentifiable foods were caked onto them. DVDs were constructed, Jenga-style, on the coffee table. Cornflower blue Xanax, and powdery white Vicodins, were neatly arranged in an impressively sizable smiley face next to his movie collection. The right eye, a Xanax, was missing, so I took one from the giant, smiling mouth, to replace it.

"Dip. Hey, Dippy." I nudged him in the shoulder with my toe, and finally graduated to using my entire foot.

"Don't make me actually call you your name."

He slowly opened his eyes, blinked a few times to adjust, and settled his gaze on me.

"Hey," he rasped. His hand automatically landed on his head so he could gauge the state of his hair. All three of us spawn had the same blond hair, with eyes in various shades of blue. Abby was navy, I had periwinkle, and Dippy was more on the turquoise side, depending how the light hit. "What's good, Pipe?"

"Nothing." I shrugged. "I mean, you know. Same old, I guess."

"Mhm." His eyelids drooped, but he managed to smile sleepily at me.

"Tired, huh? How long've you been sleeping?"

"Dunno."

"It's dark out."

"Huh," he grunted.

"Yeah. And, like, a crazy storm is approaching. So you'll be super-safe down here." I stuffed my hands in the pockets of my sweats.

"Thanks for the warning."

"Sure."

"How was your day, Pipe?"

"You know. The usual."

"Hm. Need something? I got a few twenties in my *Reservoir Dogs* DVD case. And a joint in *The Matrix*."

Dippy stashed different items in his DVD cases, according to theme, only he thought *Half-Baked* was too obvious for his joints.

"Um, nah, Dip. Just wanted to see you. Thanks, though."

"Yeah? Well, hey, I'm honored. But gimme just a few more hours, okay Pipe?"

"Okay, Dip. Have sweet dreams."

Dippy rolled over on his side, facing away from me. I threw his camouflage comforter over his pale, thin body. I spied a framed photograph on his end table. It was two years old. Staring back at me was twenty-three-year-old Dennis Marino. He was a muscular jarhead wearing this massive, shit-eating grin. Next to him was twenty-year-old me, my eyes all red and puffy from crying. My shoulder was hooked in the crook of his arm. He had been tugging me closer to him, and I remember not wanting to let go. The sky had been bright blue, and there was a plane behind us, waiting to take him away. I wasn't supposed to be on the tarmac, but we had a blow-out the night before, and I had to make amends. My dad snapped the picture as I was telling Dippy how brave he was, and how he was my hero. Back in those days, my brother still had his right leg.

I glanced down at the covered form beneath the camouflage blanket. A head. Two arms. A torso. One leg.

"Dip?"

"Yeah?"

"Semper Fi, Corporal."

"Oorah, Private."

"Sleep well, Dippy. I love you."

My brother was lightly snoring, signaling the end of

our conversation. I ascended the steps and ventured into the kitchen. It was obnoxiously apple-themed. We were not country people, so I never understood my mother's obsession with the fruit. An apple table cloth was adorned with apple placemats. In the center of the table, was an apple-shaped bowl, filled with glossy wax Honeycrisps.

"It's almost ready," Mom grumbled.

"Okay." I did my best to suppress a grimace. It was tuna casserole night, because she insisted that we follow the rules of lent. It meant not eating meat on Fridays. I didn't know why we couldn't order a pizza, instead, like most other Catholic families did. But, a quick glance at the refrigerator, littered with bills under gaudy, clunky, apple-shaped magnets, was my answer. We were behind on our payments. Again.

"Your father's doing overtime tonight. He won't be home for a little while."

"Okay."

"Can you say something besides 'okay'?"

"Okay." I smiled at her, attempting to make her crack a grin.

She didn't.

"Listen, Piper, there's just no easy way to say this. I know registration is coming up, but you're gonna have to take off next semester, and maybe the one after that."

"What?" I loved my community college; it was my escape.

She tucked a cigarette in between her chapped lips and avoided eye contact. "I... we... need you to work full-time to help with the income."

Mom's words, coupled with the rancid odor the oven was emitting, made me nauseous.

"Denny is in no condition to get a job," she continued. "I'm gonna start doing nights at the clinic, instead of afternoons. I'll get three extra hours that way. Your father works full-time, and he does the furniture moving on the weekend. It just isn't enough, anymore. We can't afford the tuition right now, and we need to keep Abby in St. Isadore's."

"Okay." The word escaped my mouth. I was dazed.

"Piper!"

"Shit, sorry."

My mother looked rough. She had deep creases in her forehead and purple bags under her eyes. Her hair hadn't been cut or dyed in months, giving her a strange, two-tone style. The gray roots transitioned into dark blonde, and her mane was shoulder-length and scraggly. She never laughed anymore. I couldn't even remember the last time I saw her smile.

After placing the hot Pyrex casserole dish atop the stove, Mom scooped a steaming blob of fishy barf onto a plate, and handed it to me.

I spooned the mushy dinner into my mouth. It tasted the way I imagined wet cat food, sprayed with Lemon Pledge, which has been baking in the sun for eight hours, tastes.

"How is it?" she wondered.

"Good," I lied. "Um. Lemony."

"Yeah." Mom leaned back against the kitchen counter, blowing smoke at the ceiling fan. "I used real lemon this time, instead of the artificial shit."

"Cool." I bit down on something crunchy and my gag reflex kicked in. Using my thumb and forefinger, I extracted a shard of shell from my mouth. "Oh, you added hard-boiled eggs."

"Your father likes them."

"Okay."

"Piper!" My mother frowned and exhaled more smoke.

"Huh? Oh, right. Sorry."

"Jesus, you have the memory span of a fucking goldfish."

"Hey, Mom, just don't worry about everything. I mean, anything."

She raised a brow at me, probably unsure that she had heard me properly.

"I... I'll do what's best," I promised. "'Cause I love you. All of you."

"Well, you're in a peppy mood today," she commented.

"Not particularly."

"I'm sure Monsignor Lucas'll let you work full-time. They always need a receptionist."

"Okay."

"Again!"

"Oh, right. I'll thumb through a thesaurus later," I commented.

"Abigail!" Mom yelled. "Dinner! Come bring a plate to your brother!"

I heard Abby's white, patent-leather little heels click along the dining room's hardwood floor. When Mom's head was turned, I seized the opportunity, and discarded dinner into the trash.

"Goodnight." I put my hand on Mom's bony shoulder, just for a moment, and trudged up to my bedroom and closed the door. Behind it, I could hear the kitchen television, all the way from downstairs. Abigail's awful music continued there, and it went silent for a moment as the phone rang. I could hear my mother talking.

"Piper!" Mom's screech, crystal and loud, bounced off my walls.

With a groan, I went back downstairs and took the cordless into the dining room. Receiving phone calls was a rarity.

"Hello?"

"Hey, Pipe." Dad's voice, though gruff, was the most cheerful one I had heard all day.

"What's up, Dad?" I smiled.

"Just wanted to know if you needed anything. Gonna stop by the pharmacy for Denny's medicine."

Finally, I thought. *My first normal conversation of the day.*

"Thanks, Dad, but I went shopping yesterday. I lo—"

"Oh, hey, kiddo, I forgot to tell you—need to postpone the soccer match. Unless you wanna go without me. I got a job. Uptown Manhattan. Some kind of ballroom.

You should see this baby grand. We should be able to pay a few bills with this one."

I pinched the bridge of my nose and closed my eyes. We had been planning the match for the past three months. Freedom Island Strikers were playing an international friendly. I knew that we would lose, but it didn't matter.

"No problem, Dad." I pressed my cold palm against my blazing forehead, and let my lids droop closed. "Just be safe getting home. A storm's coming."

"Yeah. Terrible one. Better get off the phone. See you in a few, kiddo."

"Bye, Dad."

I hung up and put the phone back on the charger. The television was back at full volume. I glanced in the kitchen. Abby was sitting beside Mom at the kitchen table, being spoon-fed macaroni and cheese, because Abby refused to taste the casserole. Feeling my love, like my stomach, curdling, I went back up to my bedroom, and once again closed the door.

2

Locked and Loaded

I OPENED UP THE balcony doors, and a gust of chilly wind carried in the thick smell of ozone. The dark sky's clouds rolled rapidly. I could feel the storm approaching; thunder was on its way. With that kind of atmosphere, gloomy and hopeless, I figured it was a suitable time as any to off myself. I was waiting for the opportune moment to do it, and there was no better time. Without me, it was less expense for the family. No extra mouth to feed. No clothes to purchase, no tuitions to cringe about, no expensive textbooks to put on the charge card. Dennis would have Abigail. She would have him. My parents would have them. My family would survive. And I wouldn't have to be let down, or ignored, or disliked.

I cleared my computer of its internet history and pass-words. The last thing my folks needed to do was have in-stant access to my blog, *Piper at the Gates*, where I posted suicidal poetry on a daily basis. Some gems included, "Put pennies over my lids when I close my eyes; I have to pay the fare when I die; Ferry me away, Charon, after my goodbye; I promise there's no need for you to cry; Stay away from whiskey and rye."

Other websites I frequented were lists of the best ways to kill oneself. The first one I clicked on urged the desper-ate to snuff it in unique and fun ways. I never knew there was a fun way to die. The site implored, "Be creative. Go out in style. Leave a mark. Let people talk about it for a long time to come." I figured I never drew attention to my-self to begin with, so maybe going out with a big bang would be the missing exclamation point at the end of my life's sentence.

The options included luring a grizzly bear to your meat-covered body so it would maul you to death, extract-ing your intestines via an incision in your stomach, and lighting yourself on fire. Apparently overdosing on sleep-ing pills, slitting your wrists, and blowing grey matter all over the bathroom wall with a Glock was *so* out of style. I thought about maybe smoking myself to death, but didn't have enough money to afford a carton of cigarettes. Besides, it had to be a crapshoot. If I didn't expire, I'd get stuck with a wheezing cough. It would last for days and days.

I didn't have heroin, but I didn't want to stick a needle in my arm to begin with. There were no extra painkillers, either, and I wasn't going to dip into Denny's necessary stash. I couldn't drink myself to death, because there was no liquor in the house. We didn't own a piano, so taking the wire to decapitate myself wasn't an option. There was the possibility of stealing Dippy's old Confederate flag t-shirt, and visiting Harlem with it on, so I could get beaten to death. But I loathed racism, and it wouldn't be right to push someone into being a murderer, anyway.

Asphyxiation by way of vomiting was disgusting, though it would have been a stellar homage to AC/DC's Bon Scott, Led Zeppelin's John Bonham, and the brilliant Jimi Hendrix. I didn't know if drinking household cleaning products would do the trick, or if they would just burn the fuck out of my esophagus. Anything that might cause me to regurgitate my mother's tuna casserole surprise was out of the question.

I mulled over movie suicides, but I wasn't exactly sure if they would work in a real-life situation. Alex survived in *A Clockwork Orange*, after all. So did the Narrator in *Fight Club*. I could go all *Girl, Interrupted*, but I didn't like my neck being touched, so hanging from a shower rod was not something I was willing to try.

I dialed the 800 number on my cell phone.

"This is the Suicide Hotline."

"Hi!" My voice sounded foreign; abnormally high and cheerful, as if I was going to place an order for a birthday cake.

"Are you thinking about committing suicide?"

I pictured the guy on the other end, sitting at a desk with some Cup-A-Noodles, thumbing through a Bible, or going over his crisis intervention script. His voice was gruff and tired-sounding. He had a non-regional diction. I wanted to peg where he was from, but it was futile. After all, he would be the last person I spoke to before I died. He was probably named Jim, or John, or Jeff, and ordered two scoops of vanilla at Baskin Robbins instead of trying the other thirty options. I was strangely comfortable with the thought.

"Umm." I bit down on my lip. "Yeah. Yes. Totally thinking. But, um, I'm actually, you know, gonna go through with it. This isn't one of those 'talk me out of it' calls or anything."

I tucked the phone between my shoulder and my ear as I tidied up my bedroom. I yanked the bedcovers into place, fluffed the pillows, and neatly stacked the paperwork on my desk. When I had decided I was going to exterminate myself, I spent hours writing notes divvying up my earthly possessions. I left the paperwork for the arrangements in a manila envelope.

I was to be cremated. I hated fire, but it was to be the

less expensive route. My parents didn't know I had already purchased a "Limited Service Cremation Package." After all, I was an adult. It included the cremation, to be done immediately, and with no public viewing. The ashes would be picked up at the funeral home or delivered to their home. Since the funeral home was not involved in arranging any type of memorial or graveside service, there would be none. They could do whatever they wanted with my ashes: scatter them, keep them, or toss them. I didn't care. I would be dead, probably hanging out with Old Lady Hennessey, in just a few hours.

The bill came out to two grand. I had it covered. Over the course of about six years, I stashed money in Dippy's hollowed-out high school chemistry textbook. The cash I received from birthdays, graduations, holidays, and rare allowances, went straight into the book. When I started working part-time and had expenses to pay, whatever was left over at the end of the week got added to the pot. My ultimate goal with it all would have been to take a vacation to New Zealand, just to get as far away from home as possible. But my fun money became my death money.

"Do you have a plan?" The suicide helper guy's voice brought me back to reality.

"Actually, that's why I'm calling."

"What, ah, do you mean?"

Outside, I heard a roaring thunderclap.

"I need the right plan. Oh, um, my name is Piper, by

the way. What's yours?"

"Piper, my name is Jerry."

I knew it had to be a J name. Jerry. Jerry, who eats vanilla ice cream. Two scoops. Sugar cone. Jerry, who reads all of the Bible, and not just the crazy Leviticus stuff. Jerry, my temporary friend. The last voice I would ever hear.

"Listen, Jerry, um, I've been researching these things like, you know, crazy. Here's the thing, though. I live with my folks. And my older brother. *And* my little sister. So I don't want them to have to see, or, you know, clean up anything messy." I pictured the top part of my skull being blown to pieces, since, if I had a gun, I would aim it right at my forehead instead of sticking the barrel of the weapon into my mouth. Going out like that, in a way that would mean I delivered a blow job to a pistol, was just not dignified. The top half of my head would probably be all rubble, and blood, and goo. That would create at least a decade's worth of therapy for the other four people occupying my home. And someone would have to clean it up, too. No one deserved all of that mess for my termination.

Jerry said, "Just–"

"Did you know Jack Daniels died from a toe infection?" I sat down on the edge of my bed and glanced at my toe, wiggling it. I had painted a peace sign on it.

"I did not know that, Piper."

"I don't have time to wait around for a toe infection to kill me, you know?"

"Piper, why do you want to kill yourself?"

"I always just... wanted to go out on my own terms. Plus, I don't want to see my family unfold because of me. You know, um, I got fired from my job and no one knows. But that's just, you know, the final nail and all. Things have been building."

"What kinds of things?"

"My brother's a veteran. He got his leg blown off in Iraq."

"I'm sor—"

"I know. I mean, thanks. Everyone's sorry, you know?"

"Okay," he croaked.

"That was bitchy of me, Jerry. I'm sorry."

"No, no. It's not a problem."

"And my Mom, like, had me do most Mom things. Taking care of my kid sister, and there was no one else to cook, or clean, or buy groceries. Now that she nixed her crazy manic hobbies, she's trying to be Super Mom and, like, stepping on a lot of toes. I hardly ever see my dad. Oh! And, apparently, we're so broke from frivolous expenses that I have to take some time off from college, which is like, the only place I feel remotely content. Financial aid won't even work, given our income. It's just blown on... other things."

"A student loan?" Jerry suggested.

"In this economy?" I fired back.

"Scholarship?"

"Single, white, childless, middle-class female."

"Well, do you have other relatives you could, perhaps, live with, temporarily? Borrow money from them?"

"Nah." I frowned. "Grandma Flannery's the only surviving one, and she's stashed away in a home talking about how the Holocaust wasn't really real, and Anne Frank was a fictional character thought up by the Jews. We pay for half the expense of the home. And, otherwise, it's just us."

"A shelter, perhaps?"

"Oh, geez, Jerry. I'd rather die. I mean, like, literally."

"They're not so terrible—"

"A shelter? For like, wayward twenty-somethings?"

"There's always the psychiatric ward." Those two words sent a chill down my spine.

"No," I insisted. "Never. I can't be there with the legitimately batshit-crazy folks, who are all screaming and rocking back and forth, yelling at nurses for ice cream and stool softeners. My mom, she works at a clinic for disturbed people, and it's... it scares the shit out of me."

"What about—"

"Listen, Jer, I'm secure with the all of the reasons why. Locked and loaded."

I thought of Mrs. Hennessey's big blue hands. And I

thought about my sister growing up, probably getting pregnant before her senior year. I couldn't stand to see Denny staring at the switched-off television anymore, knowing how he was actually seeing the Gulf. I hated how only his dismembered mannequin body was home. Nothing much was on the inside. My mother was going to get lung cancer or emphysema from her chain-smoking. Crazy, Jew-hating Grandma Flannery would succumb to her Alzheimer's. And maybe my dad would get crushed to death by a falling baby grand.

"There are so many reasons not to," Jerry insisted.

"Yeah," I sighed. "Yeah, yeah, yeah, yeah, yeah."

"I'm serious. Piper. Let's talk this through."

"Jerry, what do you think about Nirvana?" I glanced at the poster on my door and bit my lip. Kurt was staring at me and clutching his shoe. It was black and white.

"You're a Buddhist, Piper?"

"No, I mean, you know. The band. Kurt Cobain. Grunge. Flannel shirts. The nineties."

"Oh, ah, Kurt Cobain. Yes. They're okay, I suppose. But—"

"Well," I interrupted. "In his suicide note, he wrote, 'It's better to burn out than to fade away.' And a lot of people think it was this original thought of his, but it's actually a lyric from Neil Young's song, 'Hey Hey, My My.' You know it?"

"I... think so."

"I mean, it's enjoyable. Classic rock."

"Maybe we can discuss places in your area where you can go."

"Y'know." My eyes flicked to the window. "I'm pretty sure I know what to do now. I um, just have one question, Jerry."

"Of course, Piper. But, first—"

"What's your favorite ice cream flavor? Wait, you know what? Don't tell me." I wanted to keep my idea of Jerry, vanilla ice cream on a sugar cone, intact.

I abruptly ended the phone call without letting him answer, and shut off my cell. I put Dippy's dog tags around my neck. I swiped them when he wasn't watching. When the chains were fastened, I grabbed a metal baseball bat from my closet and stepped onto the balcony. I had pawned a twelve-karat-gold crucifix necklace Grandma Flannery had given me for my Sweet Sixteen, for the bat. Mostly, I just liked having something to protect me at night.

The rain was falling sideways, and I was drenched within seconds. With the bat high above my head, I tilted my face up at the sky. The last thing I remember was the sound of a frighteningly loud crack, an amplified buzzing in my ears, and a flash of the brightest white I had ever seen. I smelled smoke. And then everything faded away.

3

Welcome Back

WHEN I OPENED MY eyes, I squinted so the harshness of the light wouldn't hurt so much. It was like when I would go back inside after spending hours and hours in the snow, only reversed. Instead of seeing dark, I saw light. Lots of it. Somewhere in the distance, I heard soft, slow, rhythmic beeping, but I paid no attention to it. The sense of sight was more important to me than sound. Heaven was foggy, and I wanted to see it clearly.

As my eyes finally adjusted, a tall, curvy black woman, dressed in all white, completely filled my line of vision. She wore a white headband secured in her wild, curly hair. Her teeth were almost blinding when she smiled at me.

Around her neck was a delicate, glittering gold crucifix.

She was my guardian angel. And she was lovely. She had full lips but did not paint them with any stupid color. They were natural, with a slight rosy color filling them in. Her cheekbones were high and well-defined. My angel had the smoothest skin I had ever seen, and it radiated a shiny glow. If I hadn't known any better, I would've thought she was slathered in cocoa butter.

I gaped at her.

"Piper Marino." She smiled. "Welcome back."

Her voice was delicate wind chimes on a spring afternoon. I desperately wanted to hear more of it. I wanted to grab her hand and ask her to lead me to Grandpa Flannery, and Grandma and Grandpa Marino, who I had never had the chance of meeting. I wanted to ask her if you used the bathroom in the afterlife or not, because I didn't feel the urge to go. In fact, I didn't feel hungry, either. I was thirsty, though, but it was probably because I was filled with both excitement and nerves.

More importantly, I had to ask if Mrs. Hennessey was there, or if she went to the other place. I wanted to book an appointment with Jesus, and Buddha, and Gandhi, if they were there. And, most importantly, Kurt Cobain. I needed to speak to him immediately. I also wanted to set up a television package where I could watch my parents and siblings from my new residence in Heaven.

Still smiling, the angel told me how some special people wanted to see me. I was only dimly aware of my body—or soul—whichever it was. I was filled with excitement. Grandpa Flannery died fifteen years ago, and he was always so much fun to be around; he had always been red-faced, singing his Irish drinking songs. He let Dippy and I have our first taste of beer when we were just kids. Whenever we visited his grave in the cemetery, I left notes and Irish flags. Dippy, being Dippy, left cigarettes and mini bottles of booze. Abigail never knew him, so she just dropped a flower and ran off to chase butterflies.

"Are you ready?" The angel glowed.

I nodded excitedly, and she stepped aside.

It wasn't what I wanted to see. In fact, it was what I feared the most. I recoiled in horror.

My dad's giant mug came into view; he appeared scared and ashen, his focus switching from me, to Mom, who was pacing until my angel took her shoulders and guided her to me. She needed a smoke. I saw Abby in her stupid dress, and her large moon eyes were all red and puffy from boo-hooing. Dippy was in his wheelchair, not wearing the prosthetic leg he had to pay for out-of-pocket. He appeared more shaken than the rest of them.

Somewhere to the side of me was an Easter basket, flowers, and tremendous pastel balloons. I saw them with my peripheral vision. Heaven had a weird welcome package.

"Pipe? Piper!" Dad yelled. "CAN-YOU-HEAR-ME?"

"Sir." My angel cringed. "I can assure you that she hears you."

Mom flew over to me. It seemed like she hadn't slept in days. The usual dark circles under her eyes were air bags deployed after a massive three-car-lane collision. I couldn't tell whose skin was grayer—hers or Dad's.

I flicked my oculars over to Denny, though my vision was mostly obscured by my mother's cleavage. It would have been kind of funny if she wasn't smothering me, and hysterically babbling in Tongues.

"Mom!" Denny yelled. He wheeled over to us, trying to get her to stop suffocating me.

"I'll take care of it," the angel promised. She was working diligently to pry my crazy mother off of me.

I wanted to ask what the hell my family was doing in Heaven. They were not supposed to be there with me. It was me who died. Unless the lightning caused the house to go on fire. Immediately, I was sick.

I coughed, overwhelmed with nausea; and, instantly, there was a mucus-yellow cup at my mouth, with a blue bendy straw sticking out of it.

"Drink," Mom commanded. Water sloshed over the sides. Her hands were shaking. I wasn't sure if it was because she was having nicotine fit, or if her nerves were completely and utterly killed. Could dead people have nicotine fits?

For a moment, I thought how maybe I was in Purgatory. But the bright white light indicated otherwise. Unless we were merely in a waiting room.

I wanted my angel to take care of me, and give me my drink, because I was sure she wouldn't be such a mess. She was calm, and not crazy.

I wrapped my lips around the straw and sucked, feeling immediate relief as the water filled my mouth. My tongue unstuck from the roof of my mouth and my throat was lubricated, which it desperately needed. The water was ice cold, almost metallic, when it collided with my tastebuds.

"Well," the angel chimed. "I can see she's in capable hands now. Piper, if you need anything, you just call for me. Alright?" She pointed to the right side of her chest, where a piece of laminated paper dangled. "Arella's the name, honey."

Arella. Arella the angel. How was I going to call for her if I didn't know how? Just yell her name? But my vocal chords were paralyzed.

And then Arella the angel was gone.

I peered back at my family and frowned. Though I felt horribly guilty for what I did, I was tired of being in the waiting room, and just wanted to make the eminent crossover. Grandpa Flannery was waiting for me, and I was confident that Arella would take me there whenever I could go.

"Mommy," Abigail whined. "Why isn't she talking?"

"She's probably just feeling a little traumatized, Abby," my dad answered. "Besides, she might have just a teensy tiny bit of damage. Nothing to worry about, though."

Abigail gaped at me, her facial features screwing up the way they did when Denny forced her to try sour candy. I wondered, for a moment, what was going on. I was afraid to know.

"How long is she going to have the scar?" my little sister inquired.

Alarmed, I widened my eyes and glanced down. Scarring? How could there be scars of any kind in the afterlife? I noticed how only my arms were visible because of the cheap, itchy, white-and-blue linens they stuck me in. How odd. I was expecting silk, and full, feathery wings.

My mother quickly diverted her eyes away from me, and moved her stare down at the floor. I glanced at Dad and Denny, and saw how they were doing the same. But Abigail's focus was locked on me. She terrified me with her stare. I wanted to tell her how she was being such a little Damien, but I couldn't bring myself to speak. Though I knew the words in my head, I was having trouble getting them out. It was so frustrating; I just wanted to scream at Abby, but the words would not come out of my mouth. With a fierce determination, I opened my mouth. I focused clearly on the letter, and then the whole word. But it was impossible to spew it out.

My folks always liked to tell the story of my first

word. Apparently they had playfully argued since the first day I was born about what my first word would be. They even took a bet on it. Of course, Dad chose the word "daddy" and Mom chose "mommy." Denny, two at the time and already speaking for a year, believed my first word would be "poop."

When I was almost a year old, the momentous day had finally arrived. Though I don't remember it, my parents had been videotaping me every day since I'd begun to babble incoherently, and constantly, at six months.

We were all gathered in the living room, and my dad had aimed the old video camera at me. It had weighed a ton back in those days, so he had to steady it on his shoulder. My mother'd been sitting on the floor, me on her lap, and her arms were folded around me. She was so young. Mom had a dusting of freckles across her pinkened skin; and, the blonde hair Dennis, Abigail, and I sported, was inherited from her. We all had her blue-based eyes, too, though Abigail's were much darker than anyone else's. Dad had the Italian features—hazel-blue eyes and brown hair. He, like how Denny used to be when he saw sunlight on a daily basis, had olive skin. I was glad that I got Dad's mouth; it meant a wide, toothy smile.

"Are you ready to talk, pretty Piper?" Mom had asked. Her head was tilted down toward mine.

She'd worn a fuzzy sweater with a stitched kitten on

it, and acid-washed black jeans. Her glasses were large, rose-tinted red octagons. Nothing about the era was appealing.

In those days, we had shit-brown shag carpeting in the living room. The television was a small Sony. It had been placed in a wood entertainment center my dad built. It had been an open china closet with the television, a twenty-seven-inch, in the center; the VCR was on top of it, and the newly-purchased cable box was on top of that. The rest of the entertainment center had been occupied by a miniature stereo, and about a hundred cassette tapes. There were only about three VHS tapes—cartoons recorded from the television, my parents' wedding, and Denny's and my baptisms.

We never had any top-of-the-line stuff, but it didn't matter. Who needed a fireplace, anyway? And, for that matter, those crazy computer things that people had been talking about did not interest my parents whatsoever.

Mom had been a stickler for the typewriter; not the electric one, but the manual Remington kind. She always commented on how she liked to pound down on the keys, and how it was a therapeutic feeling. It sounded insane. Her fingertips would be bruised and calloused, but she was pleased.

Almost as pleased as she was when her baby girl had been prepared to say her first actual word.

"Say 'Mommy,'" she had cooed. "Mom-my. Mmmommy. Mommy!"

Little Dippy stepped in front of the camera. He'd been wearing swimming trunks, since it was July, and Dad hadn't wanted to turn the central air on, so we could save on bills. We hadn't had a pool back in those days—not a real one, at least—but Mom had picked up one of those hard plastic mini-pools for poor kids like us who didn't know any better.

Denny's smile had always been infectious. With his dimples, and wide, goofy grin, you couldn't help but fall in love with the kid. He had straw-blond hair, and eyes, almost matching my own.

"Dad!" he'd screamed. "Dad! Look!" Little Dippy had been hopping up and down like a deranged kangaroo that sniffed way too much nose candy. His arms flailed, his cheeks were bright red, and he'd been unrelenting in his bid for attention.

"Jesus Christ, son, get out of the way for a minute, will you?" Dad grumbled.

You couldn't see him on the video because he was taping, but all throughout my childhood, my dad had worn the same thing all the time when he was home: a white undershirt, which he called his 'guinea tee' and old denim jeans, frayed and torn. His glory jeans, as he'd called them. From his glory days. Woodstock had been a major deal, apparently.

"Bruno, language," my mother'd hissed. "Dennis get

the *hell* out of the way."

Denny stopped his insane hopping. He'd stood, frozen, in front of the camera for a moment. Then he'd thrown himself on the floor front-first.

"Hell," I said.

My family had stopped and stared. The bickering went silent. Denny stopped feigning death.

"Did she just, ah, say what I think she said?" asked Mom. She had appeared half-amused, with her grin cocked to one side.

"Think she did," Dad agreed.

Denny, his jaw touching his chest, peeked at me in bewilderment.

"It was a boo-boo word." His eyes had grown huge; two dinner plates. "How come I'm not allowed to say that?"

"Because it *is* a boo-boo word," Mom had giggled. "Did you get it, Bruno?"

"Yeah. Yeah, I got it," he'd chuckled. "Shit, can't believe her first word was 'hell.' Guess we can't send out letters and call people with that kinda information, huh?"

From there on out, I had learned a flurry of swear words. Hell was the first, damn followed, shit was shortly thereafter, and fuck was the crowning swear.

I had tried to absorb every word, to learn as much as I possibly could in the art of mimicking. Dippy had verbalized words like truck, milk, television, and Batman.

Dad, words like radio, condom, union, and beer. Mom, words like church, supermarket, telephone, and cigarettes.

Years later, when it had come time for Abigail to speak, her first word was "Piper."

"LOOKS LIKE SHE WANTS to say something," Dad deduced.

He kept his focus on me, his arms folded over his chest. I knew the stance well. It was what he referred to as 'deep thought,' but I think he stole the term from a book, or maybe a movie, and twisted it into what he wanted it to mean. Dad was on the mark; I did want to speak. I wanted answers for the million-and-one questions, all buzzing bees in my head.

"Hell," I wheezed, my fist pounding against my chest. "Hell! Hell! Hell! Hell!"

4

Morphine

MOM GRABBED ABIGAIL AND rushed out of the room, and Dad frantically yelled for help. Denny wheeled to my side and pushed a button.

Arella was back.

"What in the world is going on?"

I pointed to my throat and coughed.

"She spoke," Denny piped up. "Well, she kind of screamed."

"Hell... Help..." I rasped.

"Nurse!" My mother's voice boomed. "Can you do your job, please?"

I froze. Nurse? Not angel, but nurse. White scrubs.

Squeaky white rubber shoes. Identification card clipped to her top. The faint outline of a box of smokes in her pocket.

I was in a hospital. The beeping sound I heard was the heart monitor I was hooked up to.

"Fuck," I whispered. "I'm alive."

"Of course you're alive, Pipe." Dad's eyebrows darted up in confusion.

I shook my head violently, my hair whipping my face. I couldn't believe I had failed at killing myself. I failed at so much, but I thought that getting struck by lightning was a sure thing, at the very least. People die of lightning strikes all the time. Why did I have to be the one who survived it? I figured how maybe I should have extensively Googled it before I did it, and not just resorted to Wikipedia. All of my professors would have been incredibly disappointed in me.

"Maybe you should, uh, sedate her," my father suggested to Arella.

I was flailing in bed, my head continuously shaking back and forth. I must have been muttering things in the process.

"Piper, are we gonna have to knock you out?" Arella wondered. One of her hands was secured on her hip.

"No, no," I insisted. "No, please. No. No. Not necessary. I'm calm."

I raked my fingers through my hair, noticing how oily

the roots were. I had taken a shower not too long before I spoke to Abigail, so there was no reason for it to be in the state it was in.

"Well if she starts to turn into Regan from *The Exorcist* then we're gonna have a problem. For now, though, she's gonna be just dandy. Right?" Arella warned.

"Uh-huh."

"See these buttons right here?" Nurse Arella pointed to a red button the size of a doorbell to the side of me. It read, CALL. "Well, see, this one lets me know that you need me here." She gestured to a Jeopardy selector contraption. It had a thin, clear wire, snaking back to a hefty bag filled with clear liquid. "This other one, over here, is the magic button. You know why it's magic, right?"

I shook my head.

"Because it's the Morphine button. You understand what I'm trying to tell you, don't you?"

I nodded.

"You just press the call button if you need me. I'll be doing my fill of paperwork and you know that I'll be needing breaks sometimes, so don't hesitate."

"Thanks."

Nurse or not, she was an angel. When she walked off, her shoes squeaked as rubber tapped the linoleum.

"What day is it?" I wondered.

"Saturday," Dad answered, checking his watch. "Well, Friday just rolled into Saturday."

"What happened to me, guys?"

"Pipe," Dippy jumped in. "Maybe now's not the, uh, best time."

Dippy still appeared shaken. I couldn't believe how he didn't bring his leg with him, since he took it everywhere. It wasn't so much that he was embarrassed about missing it, but it was just what he was used to. His eyes were tired. I wondered if he had slept at all. Though he didn't seem to be in physical pain, I couldn't figure out what was going on inside of his head. The faded gray USMC shirt he wore was filled with wrinkles. Now, more than ever, he was just too skinny. A fondant-coated skeleton.

I pressed the Morphine button for the first time. A small push.

"Please," I groaned. "I need to know what happened."

My mother re-entered the room with Abigail, whose skin was tinged green, and set her down on Dad's lap. I knew how I had terrified the hell out of her with my screaming, and I hoped she would someday understand.

"Piper," Mom sighed. She walked over to me, and took a seat beside me on the hospital bed. "What were you thinking, going outside on the balcony during a storm?"

She didn't know.

I pressed the Morphine button.

Mom finger-combed my hair and Dutch braided it, securing it with a ribbon piece she cut off from a balloon.

My hair was long, and the end of the braid rested well below my hips. My sole purpose for growing it out was the idea that I was going to donate it to charity. The problem was, though, after six years of growing it out, I became attached to it. Abigail called me Rapunzel, and even asked if I could stand on a chair so she could climb up my braid. I declined, she got mad, and, the next morning, I woke up with a mustache drawn on in permanent black marker.

"Piper, did you hear me?" Mom asked.

"Yeah. Yes. I mean, yes, I heard you," I murmured.

I pressed the Morphine button hard, with my thumb. I was only slightly feeling doped up, and wondered why it wasn't hitting me so hard.

I looked down at the thin white blanket, draped over me, starting at my waist. With agitation, unable to exert much energy, I settled on kicking the blankets off of me, and examined my legs. Slightly grossed out by the light stubble they sported, since I hadn't bothered shaving during my shower, I quickly covered them back up. There was no scarring like Abigail had so cruelly mentioned.

"Piper! Stop fussing, will you?" Mom frowned. Her hands wrung as an indication of what she wanted to do to me. "That damn thing is on a timer, anyway. You can only get a dose of it every ten minutes."

"Really?" Immediately, my hand darted to the nape of my neck to scratch. I pressed the magic Morphine button again, just to piss her off.

Dad and Dippy were sitting on the far end of the bed. I wanted my question answered before I awarded them what they were all seeking, but it didn't seem as though I had any choice, or say, in the matter.

"Listen, guys," I sighed. I hated having the floor. "I was out on the balcony—and don't frigging say anything to the hospital people, because I don't want to get sent down to psych—because I just…" I trailed off as I thought about what I had done. Part of me wanted to keep the secret from my family. I got away with it, and could keep it under wraps, but the nagging feeling in my stomach told me to spill. Dishonesty was always such a cop-out.

"You just *what*, Piper?" asked Mom.

"Tell us, Pipe. It's okay." Dad placed his hand on top of mine, squeezing gently.

"I tried to kill myself," I murmured.

Nothing was heard in the room except the shallow breathing of five people.

My eyes were heavy, but there was no pain. I felt an oncoming migraine, but it passed. I just wasn't sure why it was so hot in the room.

They didn't even see the stuff on the table in my bedroom. Not the manila envelopes, paperwork, CDs I left out for them, or my laptop. I also thought the metal bat I used would be a fair indicator. But they knew nothing, at all, about anything.

"How?" Mom asked, filled to the brim with stupidity.

"Jesus Christ—"

"Language!"

"How? How do you think? I was holding a frigging metal baseball bat above my head. I was, uh, drenched. And I was wearing... Dippy's dog tags. I needed to be a good conductor of... electricity. You know, like, ah, a modern Ben Franklin or whatever. But... younger and without the kite."

Blank stares.

I pressed the Morphine button again. It was my new favorite hobby.

"I guess anyway you owe... no, uh, I owe Dippy tags back, Devil Dog," I babbled. Something about what I had just mumbled wasn't right, but I didn't care.

Reaching for the metal, something reminiscent to static electricity zinged my fingers. I removed the tags, and handed them back to Dippy.

"Hey, Pipe..." Dippy put the tags back around my neck. He couldn't help but chuckle when I botched what I had to say to him. "Keep 'em, please. You're my kid sister, and I want you to have them. If anyone deserves to wear those, you definitely do."

"Yeah, but, they're supposed to go to your wife, some-day."

"Pipe." He laughed again. "I don't see me getting married anytime soon, ok? But if it happens, we'll negotiate."

With the support of my dad, Dippy got close to me and pressed his lips against my forehead. It was a comforting feeling; something he hadn't done in ages. Though Dippy and I were closer than we had been before he became a jarhead, he was prone to withdrawing into himself, where, weeks on end, he would hardly ever emerge from his room.

"We need to talk when you get home," he whispered into my ear.

"Okay."

My mother clicked her tongue. Her arms were angrily folded over her gigantic chest. Her right foot was sticking out, and she tapped the toe of her shoe. If she were any angrier, she would have been sprouting horns. As it was, her face was bright red, though I couldn't be sure if it was due to anger or embarrassment. Or because I had used the word "okay" yet again. I never did get a chance to thumb through the thesaurus. Maybe I should've said, *affirmative.*

"Uhh, so," I slurred. "Please someone, um, tell... what... happened."

The Morphine's warmth made each nerve in my body hum.

I glanced at my brother, but he put his head back down.

Abigail twirled a lock of blonde curl around her thin, polished finger.

"I'll tell you," Dad croaked.

He pulled up a chair close to me and took my hand in his. His hands were rough and calloused from the work he did. I loved his hands. Dad never had clean fingernails, nor did he bother to clip or file them. If they got too long, he'd use a pocket knife to shave them down. Dad had cuts, bruises, and other markings on his large hands. Hands so gentle when he carried me as a baby. Knowing hands that put hooks on fishing poles, and worms on those hooks, just so I could catch fish. Dad's hands, rough as they were, would gently brush tears off of my cheeks when I cried. Those tear-catching moments were so gentle that it was as though a soft paw was doing it.

"Dad?"

"I was there, Pipe."

I had no idea he was home when the lightning had struck.

Dad moved his other mitt through the short, dark tangle of hair on his head. His olive skin was green under the awful, fluorescent lighting. None of us appeared anything like him, except for my smile, though he always told me how he and I were of the same kind. We shared the same blood type, too. My hands were fair at crafting, but they could not hold a candle to the things he could do with a knife and some wood.

"What happened, Dad?"

"Basically." He ran his hand through his hair again. "I

pulled up with the truck, glad to finally be home because it was pouring out there. Even started hailing, you know. And what do I see when I get out of the truck, but my oldest daughter on her balcony, collapsing. I saw just a glimpse of the lightning and then I figured it must've got you. And it did, didn't it?"

"Yeah," I rasped. My voice was barely audible. I was so thirsty but too tired to ask for some ice water. But there were more important things on my mind.

Why didn't I die?

"Dad came inside and started screaming about how you were struck by lightning," Denny picked up the story. "I heard him from all the way downstairs. So I just made my way up as much as I could, didn't even bother with the leg. Sat down in the upstairs wheelchair while Dad carried you downstairs, and Mom tended to you." He put his head down and covered his face with his hands. I saw the rhythmic up-and-down of his back.

I hated when Denny cried.

"Dippy," I softly said, "I know you would've been there, if…"

"If I could've," he finished. His voice was foreign. Dark.

"Don't worry about it, Corporal. General Dad, and Colonel Mom, here, took care of things. I'm here… I'm alive. Heart pumping blood and all."

He was about to say something else, but Mom stopped

him.

"Your father performed CPR and I called an ambulance. We got you breathing for a few minutes until help arrived. I stayed behind with Abby, but Dad and Dennis went into the ambulance with you," Mom explained.

I grinned at my dad and brother. I didn't care if it pissed my mother off. I was feeling kind of high; almost as if I was out at sea, floating gently in the warm water of my drug-induced imagination. I was safe and loved. My two protectors. Dip and Dad.

I needed to sleep. But first I needed a drink.

"You died," Dad explained.

I wasn't in warm water anymore. I didn't feel safe.

"What?"

"You died for about a minute or two... but they got your heart going again. And they got you stabilized. But you were unconscious for a while, there." He moved his hand onto mine, gently squeezed, and released his grasp. Dad wasn't someone who got shaken up by much of anything, but I knew he was horrified. It caused me anguish to know how much I had rattled my family.

What happened when I died in those moments? I couldn't remember seeing anyone in the afterlife.

"Feels like I've been asleep for a long time," I explained. The room fell into an awkward silence and, finally, I pressed the other button—the call button so Arella would come.

She was in the room in no time.

"You look dehydrated, don't you?" Arella smiled and got me ice cold water with bits of ice. She carefully held it up to my lips, making sure not to spill a drop anywhere. "Drink up."

I smiled and drank, the frigidness of it completely satisfying me.

"You folks should be going now," Arella firmly stated. "Piper needs to be alone so she can recover. And you all need to rest, too. But you can come back later on in the morning." It worked, because they packed up their belongings. "And you, young man," Arella directed at Denny, "You especially—you haven't left her side since she arrived. Go right home and sleep. You understand?"

"Yes ma'am." A strange display I had never seen came over him. It was almost like bewilderment. I could see a cute blush creep across his cheeks. But I wasn't going to embarrass him. I loved Dippy too much to mortify him in front of anyone.

Single file, each one of them came to kiss me goodbye. Dad, Mom, Dippy, and Abigail. When they left, Arella beamed at me. Her row of pearls shone.

"Get some rest, now," she insisted. Arella reached into her pocket, fumbled for a little brass key, and opened up a metal drawer. She extracted a vial and a needle. I wrinkled my nose and braced for the sting. Arella filled a syringe with clear serum, and I wondered what, exactly, it was. She inserted into my IV, instead of my arm, or else-where on my body, so I was thankful. "This is a sedative; you should be asleep in no time at all." She held up the cup again and I drank, swallowing it down. I didn't care what she administered to me, because I trusted her.

"Nurse... um, Arella?"

"Yes, honey?" She fluffed my pillow and smoothed out my bed sheets in order to tuck me in.

I had not known such comfort since I was a baby, cra-dled in Dad's arms. It was pleasing to feel this type of se-curity again. And it only took trying to off myself in order to achieve it.

The attention was placed on Abigail as soon as she was born. I was expecting it to happen, of course. At the time, I was fourteen years old, and going through the rough teenage nonsense, but the only one I could ever talk to was Dippy, even though he was baked most of the time. So, essentially, I had no one. Abigail took up all of Mom's time, and Dad always worked. Typical middle-child syn-drome. I would probably never recover from it.

"Um." I yanked myself out of my crappy flashback. "Arella..."

"Piper?"

"I know I'm scarred. From the lightning." My words sounded slurred, as though I had downed too many beers.

"Well," she hesitated. Her hands hung limp in a plead-ing sort of way.

"I can't feel it, thanks to the Morphine, but I know I have something… tissue… on me," I lamented. I hadn't wanted to say it, because saying it makes it real. "When I handed Dippy back his tags, I felt some sort of skin, uh, deviation outlined."

When Arella didn't speak, I knew I might as well autopsy my doom.

I pushed down the top of the hospital gown a few inches and gaped at my discovery. Right over my heart was a rough scar in the form of an upside-down question mark. I hadn't ever seen anything like it before. It was hot to the touch and felt like when I would scrape up my knees, and, a few hours later, I had long, thin scabs. Except my scar was thick and ugly.

"This isn't gonna help me get, um, guys, is it?" I teased. I pulled the top back up.

"Never know." Arella nervously darted her eyes around the room. I could see the faint outline of not just cigarettes in her pocket, but rosary beads. And her fingers were moving over them.

"Not so greusome," I light-heartedly stated. "Scars heal, even the worst kinds, in time."

I was beginning to feel high, with heavy lids, and a newfound appreciation for things soft, warm, and fuzzy. The blanket had to make due. When I re-focused my eyes, I noticed that Arella was smiling, though her eyes were misty.

"Hey, don't cry, Arella. You know, you're a lot like, um, my personal angel."

"I think it's about time you get some rest, now."

"No," I insisted, "I mean it." My eyes closed as my body prepared for its descent into REM.

"I know you do," Arella beamed. "You're perceptive enough. I'm your Guardian Angel."

"Sure," I nodded. I allowed myself to slip into the enveloping warmth. "That works."

"You bet your little Irish-and-Italian behind—with the heart-shaped freckle on the right butt cheek—that it works."

"How'd—"

"And," she continued, cutting me off. "It's wonderful to finally talk to you again, let me tell you. You haven't been able to see me since you were wearing pigtails. But we can talk about it later. Now, have sweet dreams. I promise we'll have time together, in the morning and otherwise."

"But," I murmured, my head slowly falling onto my shoulder.

"You heard me, Piper Angela Marino, Confirmation name Lily."

"Lily's on my chart?" I wondered, my eyes having trouble staying open.

"No," she laughed.

"You seri—" and I was dead asleep.

5

Game On

I WAS DREAMING. IT was dark and earthy. Around me were trees; high, large, intimidating trees, swaying of their own volition. The trees spoke to each other by creaking branches, the shuffling of their leaves, and, perhaps, even a silent language expressed through the roots. They had energy pulsating through their core; even the bark contorted into something resembling a face—or, well, millions of them. But they kept still, and I was not afraid. The sounds I heard were the gentle *whoosh*ing of wind, ruffling a leaf here or there, and the groans of the branches. Mostly, though, the most apparent noise I heard belonged to me: my breathing.

I was sitting on a lush expanse of dark green grass. Above me, the sky was black, though it did not encompass the perimeter of the forest-land I was sitting on. It was a lustrous black, and was splattered with twinkling, glowing stars. They were a source of comfort; in fact, they reminded me of the glow-in-the-dark stars I fun-tacked to my bedroom ceiling a few years ago, only the ones hanging in the midnight sky were so much brighter.

The earth was slightly dampened; though, it was more like light mist had settled everywhere. The air was heavy, clean, and carried a gentle, mild smell of incense. That, coupled with the scent of the lush grass, left me feeling relaxed. Even my skin was rejuvenated from the dew. It wasn't such a lousy place to visit, except for the whole black sky thing that appeared permanent.

"And, so, we meet again," a male's voice, from behind me, drawled. It was rugged—but smooth—and deep.

I swiveled around, and flicked my eyes up. I felt frightened by the appearance of someone else. Someone who I had never seen before, even if he thought otherwise. Behind him, adding to the intimidation, was a colossal, wrought-iron, black gate.

The stranger was about a foot taller than me. His eyes were a sharp blue, almost like mine, but his were far brighter. They were strangely metallic, and the irises around his pupils were a pale blue, almost white.

I had never seen anything like him in my life.

His height was only amplified by his muscle mass; he was around two hundred and thirty pounds of pure, solid muscle. He had a narrow waist, leading to a tight, six-pack of abs. The muscles weren't popping out or bulky; he was leaner, probably meaning better reflexes. He was wearing only odd, black cloth shorts, which were fringed when they got to his thick, meaty calves.

Whereas Arella was African-American and had rich, mocha skin, this guy was white in a Caucasian sort of way. But a different sort of white. He was tanned. No; he was bronze. The man's arms were completely covered in sleeve tattoos, most of them were skulls, and the nape of his neck and across each shoulder were also decorated. They contrasted brilliantly with his russet skin.

His nose was somewhat narrow at the bridge and then slowly widened out toward the bottom, leaving him with something resembling a bull's nose; it was a sharp contrast to my shorter, button nose. The stranger had full lips, though the top was thinner than the bottom. He sported one of those dimples in his chin. They were obnoxious on everyone else but him.

My favorite part of him, though, was not the killer body. Not even the stone cold eyes. It wasn't the nose, or the short, almost-buzz, of his hair. It was his ears. They were elfin to a degree.

After scrutinizing his appearance, I realized he had spoken to me.

"Sorry?" I said.

"For what?"

"Sorry for... um, not answering right away."

"It happens. I know what I look like." His voice was velvet.

I thought, *wow. Cocky.* I decided to ignore his remark, despite him being absolutely correct.

"You said we were meeting again?"

"I said, we meet again."

"Same difference, right?"

"No," he grumbled.

"Um. Anyway, we've never met. I'm—"

"Piper; yes, I know."

Who did this dream man think he was? Moreover, this was *my* dream, meaning that whatever I wanted was law. My brain, my rules. This character just needed a swift kick, so I could move on to happier dreams.

"Listen, you can leave now," I told the dream intruder. "Crazy lucid dreaming. Normally I wake up by now... you know, when I realize this is a dream."

And he did something I would not have expected: he grinned.

"Why the hell are you smiling?" I demanded. "This is my dream. Get out!"

"Piper, Piper, Pi*per*," he dragged out the syllables as invisible string pulled up his lips, forming a grin-snarl hybrid.

"Yeah, that's me. And, um, you are?"

"Lucian."

"Lucian… what?"

"It's just Lucian."

"Oh." I chewed on the inside of my cheek. "Like Prince?"

"No."

"Maybe we've just gotten off on the wrong foot and—"

Before I had the chance to finish my sentence, Lucian's trashcan-lid, scary hand was grabbing my waist. He lifted me up effortlessly. We had exactly a foot of difference between us in height. My five-four was toppled by his six-four. He snaked the other hand deep into my hair, breaking the ribbon from my braid. My hair was hanging loose, and thick, with waves. I noticed how hot his skin was; white hot—it was as though he was running a far-too-amplified temperature.

"Wh—" I began, but he closed my mouth and crouched so we were eye-to-eye. Nose to nose.

"I want you," Lucian growled.

"Excuse me?"

"You're mine, and I'm going to take you." He spoke slowly and deliberately; he knew exactly what he wanted, and there was no sugar-coating it.

"Whoa, whoa, whoa," I protested. Though it was slightly difficult to push his massive Bela Lugosi hands away, I wiggled to get out of his grasp enough to get some space between us. My waist was burning hot from his grasp. "This is my dream, damnit. You can't—"

"Oh, will you shut up!" he barked. The man—Lucian—had fury rising from within; his eyes blazed, and his nose flared. He blinked, and calmness washed over him. He cocked his head to the side and I heard the *crack* of his neck. "I had you in my grip the first time you got here." It was fascinating how his voice transformed from angry and growling to almost polite and smooth; sandpaper to silk. "And here we are, again."

"Sorry to disappoint you and all." I arched a brow. "But I'm not that kind of girl, even in my dreams. Now let go, will you? You're making me burn up." A small voice in the back of my head said maybe my body was reacting poorly to the Morphine.

He paused, scrutinizing my appearance. I was mortified, how, even in my dream, I couldn't get better clothes. I was still stuck in the blue-and-white hospital gown I hated so much.

"You think I want you carnally?" He laughed; it was loud, barking, and all teeth. As he was through chuckling, he released me from his grasp. "Humorous."

I wrapped my arms around myself, mortified and sweaty.

"I've been told I'm an attractive young woman," I declared. My brows pinned together in a line. Sure, mostly it was just a few of Dip's old boot camp buddies who stopped by once in a blue moon to visit who would tell me I had gotten cuter, but still. At the very least, I was offended. More than offended. And he was laughing. I dusted myself off, finger-combed my hair, and let out a soft *hmph*.

"I see." The stranger pursed his lips and once again drank me in. His icy façade told me that he did not see any attractiveness in me whatsoever.

How were you supposed to get out of nightmares, anyway? I tried thinking about a different dream, but it didn't work at all. I did not want to spend any more time with this Lucian guy, despite his freakishly sterling genetics.

"You owe me your soul." He placed his hand over my heart and tore a piece of the gown off. I gasped and took a step back from him. The feeling of exposure caused blood to flow to my cheeks.

And there it was—my exposed question mark, covering my heart—but, for what? It had to be where the lighting had stuck me, but I thought, for sure, that it got my head.

Lucian pressed hard, with his palm, onto the scar, and my whole body burned as though I had been lit on fire. I could only think two things: One, no one had ever been so close to my naked chest before; two, he wanted my soul? Nothing made sense. Especially not the fact that his hand was on my chest; I could feel my heart pounding beneath it. I was frightened by Lucian's closeness to me. He was hovering, his lips at my neck. As best as I could, I remained rooted to the ground.

"I don't know what you're talking about with this soul thing," I finally declared.

"We're going to get your memory cleared up, and you'll see."

"I'll, um, just take a pass on all of that."

"Are you denying me?" He twirled a lock of my hair around his index finger.

"Obviously!"

He was seething; his teeth were bared, the veins in his arms, forehead, and neck were bulging and appeared to be swelling and contracting. He tilted his chin downward and stared at me with those intense eyes of his. His giant hands were clenched into anvil fists. I had never seen muscles so tight in my entire life. It was terrifying; and, yet, I couldn't deny how I was enjoying it in a sick, twisted sort of way. It was only a dream, after all.

I took a few steps away from Lucian.

"We're not through; get over here," he demanded, pointing to a spot on the ground right in front of him.

"No." I tried to fix the cloth back over my exposed flesh, but it kept falling down again. Most people just dream about being naked in High School. I was wardrobe-malfunctioning in front of a gorgeous stranger who was dead-set on hurting me.

"Let me tell you about the scar, and what it means to the both of us." Lucian's voice was dripping with confidence; there was not one ounce of questioning.

And then: "Piper. Piper Marino. Honey, you better wake up." The voice filled the entire forest. It was melodic, inspiring, and loud enough.

Lucian widened his eyes and crouched down low, his hands in defense mode.

"I'm coming!" I yelled, running as fast as I could in the direction of the voice. I took just a second to check behind me, to see if Lucian was there, and my eyes met with his. The discoveries frightened me, even if they were only a dream.

I heard his voice echo in my head. It said, *Game on.*

MY EYES SNAPPED OPEN.

The dream was temporarily forgotten.

Now that I was still alive, awakened, I saw that I had been revived.

Except it was never my goal to continue on. I wanted to die. Arrangements had been worked out so perfectly, except for the actual process of getting rid of my life.

I did die, though. I just couldn't remember it, but I was determined to figure it out.

It took a few minutes to realize where the hell I was. I glanced at the clock, a cheap white piece of warehouse bulk, and rubbed my eyes.

And I remembered my dream.

I thought, *weird*. I've dreamt of strangers before, but Lucian was terrifying. It must have been the sedative Arella administered.

To get my mind off of my dream and onto other things, I surveyed the room. The pastel-pink piece of ribbon my mother had tied my braid with had fallen off, and was on the floor beside me.

The clock read eleven. I sat up in the hospital bed, and tinkered with the buttons and levers, until I got comfortable enough within the confines of the bed. My top half was straight, upright, and supported by the mattress. I sat there, Indian-style, surveying the room: hideous mucus-yellow linens, burgundy-colored chairs, and a pale oak night table. There was probably a Bible in one of the drawers, though I was never much interested in the Big Book. Despite my passion for reading, I had no interest in visiting Leviticus. More than anything, I craved a bath; or, at the very least, a shower. A dampened sponge would have been beneficial. My skin itched and felt dehydrated.

I was still in the hospital gown.

Another nurse—not Arella—rushed in carrying a pale blue hospital gown.

"Hello!" The nurse flashed a big, toothy grin. She moved swiftly, letting nervous energy guide her.

"Um, hi."

"Let's just give you a refresher! Your eyes are so pretty, and they'll simply *pop* in this color." She attempted to grab at what I was wearing, but I pushed her hand away, wary of the stranger's presence after the startling dream.

At first, I thought she was Arella's twin, though there were some differences: the new one appeared younger than Arella, who I had pegged for fifty. She was also a bit thinner, and wore her hair pulled back into a thick pony-tail. It overflowed with wide, lavish curls. Both women had the same eyes, noses, mouths, and jaw lines. Clearly, they were related. It was possible they were sisters. Or mother and daughter.

My salvation, her wild hair still adorned with the white headband, walked in not a moment later.

"Listen, *Nurse Hael*," Arella warned. She carried a food tray into the room. "Don't you be telling *my* patient that her eyes this, and her eyes that; her eyes are gonna *pop*!"

For a minute, I stopped trying to figure out why any-one would name their child Hael, like hail, and stared at the yellow, plastic rectangle housing my meal. It must have been sitting there from the night before, or maybe lunch was just served too early, like at the nursing home. There was a sandwich of white bread with waxy cheese stuffed in the middle, an apple, a small box of two-percent milk, and the ominous, wiggling green Jell-O. How repulsive. Almost worse than my mother's rushed meals, my stomach twisted at the hospital food. I was hungry, but the sandwich alone was enough to make my appetite fade.

"Sorry, sorry," Nurse Hael muttered. She rushed into the room with a different hospital gown. Though it was thick and white, there was also a pink tint to it. It smelled like lilies.

"Let's get you out of this old one and put you in this pretty white one over here," Arella insisted. Her eyes bore into mine.

I looked down at the one I was wearing.

It was torn above the heart. Summoning up all of the bravery I could, I peeked above my left breast and, to my horror, saw the awful scar—but there was something else. A handprint: a large, Lucian-sized one that burned. My eyes widened; but, when I went to touch it, the hand-print was gone. Unfortunately, the scar remained.

Arella sat down and moved her head into her hands. I heard the distinct muffled sob I had come to know so well. Now the nurse was falling to pieces. I wondered if I was still dreaming; and, if so, how I could possibly wake. The dream-within-a-dream theory entered my mind, so I pinched the underside of my wrist. It hurt, but so did the feeling of Lucian's frightening hand squeezing my jaw. I winced.

"Arella?" I squeaked. Hotness rushed to my cheeks.

"Piper," she sobbed. "I'm so sorry. I shouldn't have given you the sedative last night. I... I didn't know..."

Bewilderment overtook my senses. I became numb.

"Momma," Hael quietly said. "She's got to know."

"She's not ready to know all of that, yet."

"But," Hael interjected. "Didn't you tell her about the other thing, last night?"

"I don't even know if she heard me. She was so doped up."

The women exchanged foreboding stares. I wanted to jump out of my skin and make my exit, any way possible. The incredible strangeness of both the dream and the hospital was making me cardio-aware, and on the verge of panic. If only I could be home, in my pajamas and in my bed, with the door locked and music blaring.

"I did hear you," I finally chimed in. My voice surprised me. "If you mean the angel story."

Both women gaped at me as though I came from nowhere, sprouted two heads—one with pink hair and the other with green—and didn't speak English. But I heard Arella loudly and clearly the night before. She had told me personal details that could have easily been common knowledge after being hospitalized. After all, when I dressed, she did manage to get a glimpse of my body. And my full name *was* probably on the records, anyway. My parents were the kind of old-school Catholics who believed that a Confirmation name held legitimate value. I hardly used it.

All I knew, for sure, was that I wanted to get out of

there, and be out as soon as humanly possible. As kind as I thought Arella was, I was getting strange, almost-stalker vibes from her.

I didn't know why anyone would do something like fake being an angel; perhaps to scare the crazy girl straight. Make the suicide stuff scary. Or, well, scarier. But maybe to give some hope to the hopeless. People like me.

Either way, I wanted to know when the hell I could be discharged from the hospital. I wasn't even going to get them in trouble, just as long as I got to leave.

When I got home, I would just take a long, hot shower. I would put ointment over my scar, and forget everything else. The dream, the hospital, the insanity. It would come time to talk about the suicide attempt, but that would just be with my family. I was lucky enough that my parents were both too proud, and too ashamed, to let anyone know how their oldest daughter was a suicide-case. With a mom that Irish, and a dad that Italian, my issues were going to be dealt with behind closed doors—our doors.

I groaned, and peered over at the two nurses.

"She said she heard you."

"She heard nothing."

"You, um, think you're an angel." I inclined my head toward Arella. "And," I did the same to Hael. "I'm guessing you do, too."

They gave me the blank stare of doom. I hated that.

"We don't think it," Hael insisted. "We know it."

"Hael!"

"It's the truth!"

"Enough," Arella chided.

"You two must be the psychologists here or something. Or maybe just the entertainment." I smirked. Hael was a little into herself, but so were most other young women her age. "But it could just be the case of two bored, yet sweet, nurses who want to help a pessimistic cretin get on the Jesus path. What is it—Jehovah's Witnesses? Sorry, ladies. Not happening. This is, like, way too much crazy for me to handle."

I imagined getting tied down to the hospital bed as Hael fanned out pamphlets from the Church of Jesus Christ of Latter Day Saints. Maybe Arella would read aloud about the joys of Mormonism. *Wait*, I thought, *were there even black Mormons?* If so, I would crack jokes about how I would consider doing it if someone paid for my mansion in Utah, so I could have a huge polygamist family with myself in charge. I'd get a few husbands to do chores for me, instead of the other way around. And, sure, I couldn't see myself with those over-elaborate, puffy Mormon styles—the hair and clothing—so, perhaps, I could set a new trend. Fashion-forward. I desperately wanted to laugh at my deranged idea, but the serious visages the women were sporting were an indicator that, maybe, I should just keep quiet, and wait for my release forms.

I wished I wasn't going to get thrown into a mother-daughter argument over angels, and Heaven, and God, or psychology and psychiatry. I was even prepared for some magic tricks, and a speech about why devoting my life to the Lord and Savior was so important. Thankfully, my fears were not realized. To my delight, Dippy wheeled into the room. He had showered, and his hair was slicked back. He even shaved off his goatee, and brought me a little bouquet of daisies.

"Looking dapper, Dip," I smiled. I was stoked to see someone familiar—not a staff member, not someone who could be mistaken for an angel, or a demon, or part of a dream.

"Thanks, Pipe." Denny shyly smiled in return. I knew how he reacted when he was in front of other women. This time, though, he wore the prosthetic and kept his cane on the back of the wheelchair. I had dubbed it "the pimp cane" and had painted flames all over it after spray-painting it a bright, vivid purple. Dippy didn't mind; he was probably hoping for camouflage, but I wanted to do something flashy. He was proud of my artistry, and joked about how I should make a living by painting canes for the walking-disabled.

I went over to him, glad to be off of the bed, and bent down, smacking my lips against his cheek. It was a relief to not be so confined.

"Mom and Dad are talking to the administration people about signing you out of here, Pipe. Said a doctor needs to see you first. Maybe get some X-rays, or an MRI, just, you know, to be safe. Probably to cover their asses. Insurance, and all. I don't know. Abby is with that friend of hers from down the block. They did the whole, you know, sleepover thing at her house last night. Abby didn't want to be in the house. They've probably been watching, uh, that one movie with the guy, you know, the one whose poster is on her wall," Dippy yapped. His cheeks burned redder than ever. He hadn't been chatty since coming back from Iraq; it was probably the most he had babbled in some time. I liked hearing his voice, even if he was more comfortable listening as other people spoke.

"Totally," I replied. I wasn't registering much of what he said beyond 'signing you out.'

"And, hey," I continued. "I had this freaky dream last night. I mean, it was totally out there. Like a ten in weird-ness. And kind of vividly real. But I'll tell you later on at home, when we have some privacy." I sent a sideways glance at the two nurses, who hastily sauntered out of the room, clearly defeated.

There were no such things as angels. If there were, they would've let me die.

"I napped. But didn't dream. Probably for the better."
He had no idea.

"I definitely wish I didn't." I frowned. "I'm pretty sure the meds fucked with me. Hey, do you want some food?" I pointed to the tray, and Dippy wrinkled his nose. He had spent his fair share of time in the VA hospital. He promised it was clean, but horribly depressing.

"Can't wait to get the fuck out of here." Dippy commented. He patted my hand.

"Yeah," I said. "I want a shower, normal food—hopefully there's no leftover tuna—and a talk with my favorite brother."

"Your only brother," Dip corrected.

"Yeah, yeah, well you're still my favorite."

"Even though I wasn't there to save you?"

"Stop it," I warned. "You know you're my hero and all, but you can't always be Super Man."

"I haven't been Super Man in years," he sighed. Dippy nervously moved his hand through his hair, and over his chin where his goatee used to be. He appeared so uncomfortable in his body; it was a stark contrast from just a few years ago, when he was at the gym every day, bulking up in muscle mass. He would eat all of the food in the refrigerator, making grocery shopping a nearly-daily activity. I swore that the more he worked out, the more his brain cells withered away. Now, he was frail and skinny, and his ribcage was clearly visible beneath his waxy skin.

"You'll always be Super Man." I smiled at him, and he returned the gesture, though his eyes were filled with worry. "Mixed with a little GI Joe."

6

Separation

WE PACKED INTO DAD'S GREEN Ford when I was released on Saturday afternoon, after a few more
tests, and signing my papers. It was sensational to be back
in my change-of-clothes my family brought from home:
the Dean's List t-shirt, and my sweats, freshly washed-and-
dried, and smelling like the sweet lavender fabric softener
Mom was so fond of.

I couldn't be happier to be out of the crappy hospital
gown. I also knew that I got lucky about not going up to
the psych ward, or getting transferred there after my confession. Hospitals were scary enough as it was. They were
sanitary to a degree, but I always felt so dirty when I

walked out of one.

Loaded with flowers, balloons, and the Easter basket that had been ransacked by me and Dippy as we waited, my brother and I sat in the back of the pickup; Mom and Dad took the front. I couldn't fiddle with the radio buttons, precisely how my mom wanted it. She and I had different taste in music; I preferred Dad's classic rock, whereas she was interested in whatever was currently popular. But, that afternoon, there was no music in the vehicle. Instead, we drove in silence for a while. Finally, after a solid five minutes of uninterrupted calm, I couldn't take the quiet anymore.

"What did you think of that nurse?" I put on my poker face.

"The older, black one?" Mom asked.

"Yeah," I answered, "Arella. The other one is Arella's daughter, Hael."

"Seemed nice enough to me." Dad was trying to hide a smile.

Dippy didn't say anything. He, instead, kept his oculars locked on the window.

I was stoked because it wasn't raining anymore. And, soon, I would be under the dark and comforting cover of night, with lots of stars littering the inky sky.

As we sat there, I moved my hand to Dippy's and entwined our fingers. In return, he gently squeezed, though his eyes were still away from me. He preferred to stare out the window.

"What do you see out there, Dip?"

"Hm? What d'you mean, Pipe?"

"Like, you know, are you back in Iraq right now?"

"Um. Well—"

From the front of the car, my mother huffed.

"Piper, leave your brother alone, damnit," she chastised. "This whole incident is because of you. Poor Dennis didn't even do anything. You're the reason why everything happened. I can't... I still can't believe you tried to kill yourself. Why would you do something so stupid? We didn't raise you like that! If you died, you would be in Hell right now. Do you understand?"

My cheeks burned bright red, and I stared at the floor of the car, feeling mortified.

"Karen," my dad warned.

"No, Bruno. Our daughter has a lot of questions to answer. I want the truth."

And I wondered, for the sake of argument, if Lucian was real, what he would have done with my soul. I didn't even know who he was; perhaps some sort of afterlife soul collector. Unless he was like Virgil, and did guided tours for the recently departed. Regardless, it was a dream. A realistic dream, but a dream nonetheless. What actually happened was that two crazy nurses decided to mess up my mind even more when I was in a fragile, confused state.

"Mom," I groaned. "Can't it wait 'til later?"

"No," she insisted. "Abigail doesn't need to hear this nonsense. And it's almost *Easter.*"

"Okay, okay," I sighed. "Where to start..."

"Start at the beginning," Dippy said.

"Brilliant idea." I beamed at Dip, and put my head back against the cushion of the seat. With a deep breath to calm any sort of panic attack, I prepared myself for the explanation. It would most likely be followed by a question-and-answer session.

"Right." I fidgeted in my seat. "I thought that getting struck by lightning was a quick and effective way to kill myself—"

"But *why* did you want to kill yourself in the first place, Piper?" Mom swiveled around in her seat and looked at me, her eyes all juiced up with the salty stuff. Her hair was hastily pulled back into a messy bun, and the purple circles under her eyes went from being airbags, to thick, down-stuffed pillows. My mother was a mess. But she still would have been even if I wasn't a suicide case.

"What did we do wrong?" she pressed.

"It's not about you guys," I lied. "I mean, not really. Remember Mrs. Hennessey?"

My family nodded.

"Bear with me, okay? This maybe won't make too much sense or anything, but whatever. I always knew how

I never wanted to be that frigging old. It's like, why would anyone actually want to live past, like, seventy-five? In some cases, it's more like sixty-five. She was a frigging hundred when she died, you guys, That's insane! She was, like, shitting herself, and had no hearing, and couldn't see."

They didn't seem to follow my logic. It was true, though. Those were the crap-your-bed years people didn't want, anyway. Those terrible Alzheimer's years spent watching *Antiques Roadshow* at full blast, and being unable to see the trinkets which sold for a grand or two, and then forgetting all about it three seconds later. The gold-fish-memory years. Life was only about eating pudding— vanilla pudding. Not chocolate. Not tapioca. Not rice. That was Grandma Flannery. And it freaked me out.

"Pipe," Dad interjected. "But, by that rationale, you had a few more decades to go. You have your whole life ahead of you." He swung a left and got onto the express-way, switched on his signal, and coasted to the far left again. "Don't you want those years? The happy ones? Graduation, a full-time job, then maybe marriage, some kids, and all of that?"

"Okay, Dad, so now comes part number two."

My mother groaned and lit a cigarette, puffing away at it. I didn't know if she wanted to cry, or smack me in the head.

Dippy pressed his forehead even more against the window. I could see his breath forming a circle on the glass. He lifted his finger, and traced the letter P onto the fogged-up part.

"I mean, you guys know how things have been hard for me. Don't you?" I wondered aloud. My eyebrows were high up in anticipation; I genuinely wanted to know their answer.

"No," said Dad, ashamed.

"Not really," Dippy sniffled. "Wow. I'm so sorry, Pipe." He turned away from the window. His eyes were red, too. "You know you can come to me about anything, right? I…" Probably remembering when he asked me to give him a few more hours' sleep, my brother closed his mouth, and contorted his visage into a grimace. I patted his hand to let him know it was okay, and that I wasn't mad at him.

"I know," I murmured. I peered at my mom.

"I know you're going to blame me."

"Mom, I'm not—"

"But I thought you just wanted to be alone more," she admitted. "You know, being in your early twenties and all. Maybe I should have listened to Abby when she said you were sad because you never did your nails anymore, and you never go out anywhere." I hoped she was feeling guilt setting in. "I thought it was just a phase," Mom continued. "Or maybe you were a lesbian."

"Oh, geez."

"Are you? Is that why? I never see you with guys."

"Mom!"

I sensed my Dad and Dippy becoming even more uncomfortable. Dip shifted awkwardly in his seat, his eyes once again flicking to outside the window.

"It's an honest question."

"No," I groaned. "I'm not. Alright?"

"All right, if you say so."

"I don't even have girls for friends, Mom."

"Exactly."

"Guys." I frowned. "It was a lot of things, okay? The Mrs. Hennessey situation always freaked me out, for one. Number two, the economy is in the shitter right now, you know? And there's zero sign of it improving. Without me, there's one less major expense. I wrote all of this down. It's up in my bedroom. I even purchased a cremation plan." I was proud of my perverse handiwork.

"You... purchased..." My mother stammered, her skin getting sort of green-tinged when she clawed her hand onto the seat of the car, and swerved her head toward me again.

"It was the cheapest one they had. You think I want to get fired up and blasted into ashes? No way. But I didn't want to be worm food either, and worm food is even more expensive! I thought about donating all of my parts to science, but chickened out. I mean, have you seen those autopsies online? Jesus, the Y-incision alone was the deciding factor."

"Piper, are you a goddamn fucking moron?" Dad asked.

"What? Dad?"

"Only a goddamn fucking moron would do what you did, and for the stupidest reasons. You wanna die? You better make it a goddamn good reason why. Abused—which you never were, in any way. Addiction—which you never battled; not cigarettes, alcohol, or drugs. Financial instability—which you don't have to worry about because we—"

"—Bruno," Mom interrupted. "That's actually... I told Piper she had to get a full-time job, and take off for a few semesters because we just can't afford the payments."

"Karen?"

"Not when Abby is really thriving in St. Isadore's!" Mom put her hand over Dad's, and he recoiled.

We were nearing the exit to our development, so I figured there would only be about five to ten more minutes of this, depending on the traffic lights. The sky was progressively getting purpler, though the purple was infused with grays and metallic silver streaks. A lovely sky for a homecoming, I supposed. Not that I would actually sit outside to watch it or anything. I itched for a shower, despite being in clean clothing.

"Goddamnit!" Dad yelled, causing all of us to jump. "Here's some truth: *you* pushed our twenty-two-year-old into suicide because of the fucking burden placed on her shoulders. What the fuck were you even thinking, Karen? Jesus Christ! Abigail is eight years old. We can send her to a public elementary, and a public intermediate. It makes no difference! At least we can send Piper to school in the meantime. Her tuition is cheap—less than a quarter of what we have to pay annually for Abigail." He was enraged. I had never seen my dad like that before, eyes bulging, nose flaring, and a pulsating squiggly vein in his forehead, visible from the rear-view mirror.

"Can we not?" I suggested in a small voice.

"But," my mother protested. "St. Isadore's is the best school here."

"You only like it because it's upper class bullshit, which our daughter shouldn't even be exposed to!" Dad shouted. "We should've defected to Our Lady of Grace."

St. Isadore's was the most expensive Catholic school in our city, and it was the largest church, too. Each and every year, the school was praised, and given top honors. The students, all girls, often went on to achieve "big deal" statuses in the city—whether it was Miss Freedom Island, or Junior Miss Freedom Island. The education itself was not as worthwhile as the education offered in the public schools. Isadore's was more of an etiquette type of place. A charm school. They had flamingoes walking around on the lavish green lawns, and the fountains were lighted so the water appeared to jet out in different colors. One uniform cost over two hundred and fifty dollars. Instead of dodge ball, the girls played tennis and learned to synchronize swim. They had afternoon tea. They learned how to walk with books on their heads, the proper way of placing silverware, and I would assume a class on how to pretend they're still virgins.

Dippy and I remained silent.

"And you, Dennis," Dad added. "There are jobs out there. Don't think you're gonna continue living in the basement forever. Don't let this thing defeat you, son. You're so much more than that."

Dad was on a roll.

"Thanks, Dad." Dippy caught a glimpse of Dad from the rearview mirror. He knew better than to say anything else—not when our father was going off on a rare, focused diatribe.

"Dennis is in no condition to work!" Mom repeated for maybe the millionth time that month. "He can't find anything suitable for him, and he's always in excruciating pain. And you remember what the doctors, um, said. About the, um, PTSD. What can he possibly do for a living?"

"He can do something!" Dad hollered. "Just because he's got an amputated leg, it doesn't mean it's the end of the world. Fuck the war that did this to him, but he's still our son. Strong as hell, too. Maybe a little confused in the head right now, but his issues can be worked out."

I glanced at Denny, feeling second-hand embarrassment for him.

"We'll see about that," Mom seethed. She smugly stuck her chin in the air, and folded her arms over her chest.

"Listen to me, Karen," Dad demanded. "Piper's going to register for her classes. Abby is going to public school, and that's the end of it. We're going to use the Isadore's money to pay for Piper's tuition. Enough of this nonsense. I know she's our baby, Karen, but we've got a responsibility to all of our kids, not just the ones who seem to need us the most." He nodded, as if it would seal the deal.

"The public schools here are garbage!"

"Dennis and Piper went to both of them, and see how..."

My mother gave my father a poignant frown.

"You okay there, Pipe?" Dad asked.

"I lost my job, Dad," I grumbled. Hot tears of shame spilled down my paper-pale cheeks.

"When?"

"Before I tried to, you know..."

"Don't worry about it."

"Dad."

"Piper. Don't worry about it."

My dad was being extremely stubborn, and it was no use to even attempt to talk him out of it when he had his mind so fiercely set on something. It was like the time when the family had to decide where to go on vacation. The options were France, which had been my choice, because New Zealand was too expensive for the entire family; Hawaii, which had been my mom's choice; Amsterdam, from Dippy's wild imagination; and Disneyland, from Abigail, who thought she was a real-life princess.

We had argued for weeks and weeks about the pros and cons of each place.

The only con about France, I'd thought, was pretentious people. But we had plenty of those in America, so it wouldn't have been too difficult to handle. Dippy'd said he didn't want to eat any snails; and, how Parisians, especially, smelled poorly. Abigail had whined about not knowing the language, but none of us did.

Hawaii was getting boring, the magazines had explained. But Mom didn't care because she'd wanted to wear a grass skirt, take hula lessons, eat dead roasted pork over a fire pit, and get 'leid' by a Hawaiian man, all as she drank fruity alcoholic beverages with speared maraschino cherries, and umbrellas in gigantic, hollowed-out-pineapples.

Dippy's choice would have probably been my second or third pick. He wanted to frequent every hash bar in the district, but there was little else that the place had to offer—except for prostitution, though we could have hired the whore to baby-sit Abby while we went on and smoked as a family.

Disneyland was boring—rides, candy, shows. We could have gotten it at Six Flags, except Six Flags was less expensive, and we wouldn't have to fly three thousand miles in order to get there. Abigail campaigned hard for it, though. One of her most notorious ways of getting in the Disney spirit was leaving one of mom's silver heels on our stairs. I had tripped over it, went tumbling down, and knocked my head against a pumpkin, which was sitting at the bottom of the step. I was left with a concussion, and my hair smelled like squashed pumpkin for three days.

Regardless of pleading our cases, Dad ended up being the deciding factor. He tossed out all of our ideas and came up with his own: a road trip to Washington, D.C. I thought it was going to be excruciatingly awful and boring. Dad said he'd chosen it because he had never been there, but always wanted to go.

Surprisingly, I loved it. I took an immediate interest in all of the monuments and pieces of patriotic art—and so, of course, did Dippy. He was highly praised when we visited D.C., and he even met up with other Marines; they went out for drinks and had a lot of fun, which thrilled me. I had joined him just once, but thought it was more of a guys' thing to do.

Abigail was the only one who wasn't too fond of the place—which, in turn, pissed my mother off. The two either secluded themselves in their hotel room, and had ordered pay-per-view movies, or just headed to the local mall for retail therapy.

At least Dad and I had gotten to enjoy the glory of D.C.. We'd haunted all the tourist spots together—The White House, monument and memorials, art shows, walls with names, pictures, and plaques. And, of course, the gift shop. He purchased an Abe Lincoln hat for me, and I wore it immediately. had always been my favorite president. I was partial to the beard, and the way he had been assassinated.

Back in the car, Mom was shooting daggers at Dad.

I nudged Dippy in the ribs, and gestured with my head over at them.

It was strange seeing them like that, since I always avoided it by locking myself in my bedroom. It made me wonder just how long the weirdness between them had been going on. I wanted to know what started it, how long it had been taking place, and what they were planning on doing.

Having Abigail wedged between them at night couldn't be helping matters. And, sure, I liked that she did it, simply for the fact that we didn't need any more kids around. But Mom was forty-eight years old, and probably well on her way into menopause. It would also explain her mood swings, and why she always appeared red.

Clearly, the Mom-Abigail dynamic was strange, and reminiscent of the days when I'd been kicked away from the popular table at lunchtime during seventh grade. I had been too weird, they complained, and talked about death all the time.

Something had to change.

When we pulled up to our house, I let out a sigh of relief. I didn't think it would feel so comforting to be home again. And, now, with the whole money issue possibly resolved, I thought how, maybe, I could give life a few more years, and nix my suicidal ideas completely. What if my dad was right—what if I did have all of those opportunities waiting for me? I had spent most of my life dwelling on morbidity. Maybe a change, a radical one, was what I needed.

"Not a shitty night." I gave Dippy a cheery smile.

"Compared to what?"

"Mom? Dad?" I opened the passenger door, figuring it would snap them out of their momentary daze.

What I heard next sent shivers down my spine.

"Bruno," Mom bitched from still inside the pickup. "I want a separation. I can't do this anymore."

"What!" Dad shouted, his face turning the entire spectrum of red.

I stood there, frozen, my hand latched onto the handle of the door. Dippy was behind me, trying to pull me away from my parents.

"The neighbors are staring out the goddamn windows." He frowned. Dippy leaned his weight—not that there was much of it—against the car.

We lived on a long residential block, where houses were almost on top of each other. We were all what I called "double-stacked," meaning the backyard was the same as the neighbor's directly behind us, separated by a lone fence. It was a palindrome of houses.

Across from our front porch was a row of identical ones, with the street acting as a divider. Our home was semi-attached, meaning that when my neighbors were having sex, my bedroom wall would shake. Even more troubling was how they were way old, and that it was impossible to hate them because they brought fruitcake over each year, along with a new doll for Abigail. It almost made me forgive them for watching *Wheel of Fortune* at full volume, bickering about what a peanut is actually classified as (it's a legume), and the crazy, animalistic noises that sonic-boomed through the thin wall insulation.

I still curse the person who invented male-enhancement pills.

INSIDE THE CAR, MY parents were huffing and puffing at each other.

"There's no reason!" Dad roared. "You would want to separate from me!"

"Don't you dare take that tone with me, Bruno," Mom bounced back. "*There* is just one reason."

I could feel Dippy nudging me in the back with his leg,

but it was car-wreck syndrome. You know you shouldn't watch, but you do it anyway, because you're far too curious about the incident.

My parents were the damage.

"Guys," I whimpered. "I'm sorry, okay? Please don't do this."

"Get in the goddamn house!" Mom shrieked. "This is none of your business."

"It's none of the neighbors' business, either," I retorted.

"Pipe," Dad groaned. "Please."

I cursed under my breath, sneered at my mother, swiveled on my heel, and wheeled Dippy inside.

7

Drama, Drama, Drama

I know, I know, I know," Dippy chanted. The two of us headed into the kitchen; he put his prosthetic on and ordered a pizza while I excused myself to take a shower. It had been the best shower of my life; I lathered up with Irish Spring, and actually got around to shaving, leaving me with completely smooth skin which didn't sport dark blonde stubble. Choosing the Freesia-scented shampoo and conditioner, I washed my hair thoroughly, and let it air dry after I stepped out of the shower. For the first time in months, I used lotion and moisturizer. The feeling of rejuvenation increased my mood tenfold. I changed into a pink tank top, with black sweatpants, and made it just as the doorbell rang with the pizza.

"Get the door!" Mom shrieked, taking a momentary breather from yelling at my father. "Your fucking food is here."

I opened the door and smiled at Riley, who had been my neighbor since we were six. He'd been delivering pizzas on weekends for the past year to pay his expenses. He, too, still lived at home with his folks. We were currently in the same Algebra class. He only needed sixty credits, he said, so he could work full-time as an EMT.

I handed him a twenty.

"Keep the change," I insisted.

"Thanks, Pipe. Are you sure?"

"Yeah. No problem. You're lightning when you deliver here."

"Only two speeding tickets," Riley boasted.

"Good thing your dad's a cop, then."

"Yeah," he laughed. "How are you?" I saw him glance down at my scar, and quickly back up again, his eyes going all deer-in-headlights.

"Superb," I lied.

"Um—what are you taking next semester?"

"Dunno yet."

"Maybe we can take an English class together." Riley smiled. "You're a lot better at it than me."

"Than I." A smirk tugged at my lips.

"See what I mean? We definitely need to synch our

schedules."

I thought about the college, and the tuition. Suddenly, the pizza wasn't as appealing as it had been.

"Maybe." I shrugged.

"Well, let me know?"

"Sure. See you later, Riley. Thanks for the fast delivery."

"Welcome. Happy early Easter."

"You too."

I closed the door and headed downstairs with the pizza to commiserate with my brother.

Dippy's room was a gigantic mess; at best, it was an explosion of different, fascinating items strewn about artistically, to capture the essence of Dennis Victor Marino, Confirmation name George.

The mattress with the camouflage comforter was the centerpiece of Dippy's room d'art. There was his druggie coffee table, of course, with each day representing a different pill mosaic. Today I noticed that he had done it up very fetchingly in a daisy, the same kind as in the bouquet he bought for me. To achieve the flower's success, Denny used the large Vicodins for petals, a few round, bright yellow Oxycontin for the center, a line of white Oxy for the stem, and several green Percocet tablets for leaves. Scattered around were jovial Xanax and Ambien faces, and colorful, round Morphine pills lined up to resemble stars and hearts.

"Mom's such a bitch," I whined. I opened up the pizza box, and set it down between us. Dippy and I sat, Indian-style, on his mattress. He was rolling a joint, and had several insence sticks burning to mask the skunky Kush fragrance. I wasn't much of a pothead, but I enjoyed a few hits every now and then. My brother kept a stash hidden under an old pile of clothes in his dresser drawer from his bulkier days. Abigail took to snooping when Denny was getting his serious REM on. The last thing we all needed was for her to either sample some, or to go running to Mom with the bag of it.

"I figured this would happen eventually," he grumbled. He licked the sticky film of the paper and sealed his handiwork. "I mean," Dippy continued, "Dad's not around much, because he's working all the time. And she's been up her own ass lately. Like, you know, even more. All of this financial shit." Dippy took a monster bite of pizza after handing the rolled weed to me.

"Goes to show you how much you're missing when you don't pay attention."

"You got it, Pipe." Denny glanced guiltily at me.

I licked my lips and brought the joint up to them, figuring I deserved some sort of escape from the insanity I had been through. We decided to get high just to have a laugh, especially after getting the devastating news that Mom was kicking Dad's ass to the curb. No one knew what the next step would be.

So I smoked.

I lit the end of the joint and took a sharp, deep inhale. The smoky, peppery thickness clouded into my throat, and I gasped in order to bring it down into my lungs, where I would get a better effect. I held it there, deep, and counted to ten. Slowly, I let it out—but not without first coughing until my lung almost flew out of my mouth.

"You know..." I immediately lost my train of thought. I chewed on the pizza crust, my mind wandering.

Dip took a hit and blew a smoke ring. Because it was Dippy, I didn't mind that he was being a show-off.

"Maybe," I tried again. "Maybe it's Lucian's fucking fault." My eyes went all wide. My jaw lowered down. I scratched my head, trying to put the puzzle pieces together.

"Who?" Dippy wondered.

"Oh..." I thought about Lucian for a moment. He was just a dream; he had nothing to do with the situation. I shook my head. "Nothing. Never mind, it was just the dream I told you I had."

Dippy and I blinked at each other in silence. It was comfortable, though, and made better by us being high. I knew our mother was still upstairs, probably making some sort of dinner for the rest of the family, in between yelling at my Dad, because she was a medicated, programmed robot. Cooking, cleaning, washing clothes, folding, and ironing. She did it all, with the help of benzodiazapines. Karen Marino, Drugged Wonder

Woman of Suburbia.

"Hey Pipe I was thinking." Dippy quickly finished his second slice.

"About what, Dip?"

"Like, you know, getting out of here. Dad said he'd pay off your tuition, so maybe me and you... we can get our own little apartment. Something small. A one-bedroom. You can have it. I'm satisfied with a couch, or an air mattress." Optimism danced in his eyes.

"Huh," I grunted. "Sure. Okay, yeah, we'll do it. But, Dip, we can't just abandon Dad."

"Oh—true. Okay, okay. Well, Dad comes with us. A two-bedroom, one for Dad, and your own private one, too. We can live close to the campus, how about that? They've got those decent, cheap, almost-rat-free condos there." Dippy grinned brightly, and grabbed a piece of paper and a pen to jot down all of his marijuana-brilliant ideas. "All Mom needs is Abby. And we can still see them all the time. It's not, like, you know, we'd be moving to Antarctica."

"True," I smiled. Taking another hit, I settled down onto Dippy's comfortable mattress, and I sprawled out on my back, attempting to occupy the whole surface area. "They told me I died, Dip. I died. And I want to know about it. Did I go to Heaven? Hell? Purgatory? Limbo? Nowhere? I'm just so confused." I sniffled, and attacked the pot again, until comfortable numbness set in. My eyes were probably blood-red, but I didn't care.

I laughed. "And if Lucian is real, then I mean I guess we're all just so fucked, because he was this fucking humongous, fucking scary guy, all gigantic and bronze, with these crazy blue eyes and... and..." I stared at the floor and saw him in the pattern of the rug. Shaking my head, I zigzagged over it with my foot, and I about-faced the other way. "Maybe death is just nothing, and maybe it's not fair that I was brought back to this. But, maybe, I was supposed to be brought back. For what, though?"

"Uh... dunno, Pipe," he muttered. "But I can't tell you how stoked I am that you're here. Maybe we all get to do one insane, fucked up thing in life. Then it gets wiped away, and we learn, and we don't do anymore fucked up things. Mine was enlisting. Yours was... you know."

"Mom and Dad's?"

"Getting married."

I mulled it over, taking a few moments to survey Dip's room. His walls were covered with posters of bands. Authentic posters, too; not just some bands that you would listen to for a few weeks, and would soon forget about. One hit wonders. Denny loved his musical groups, even if they weren't touring anymore, and even if some of them were dead. Their music, he insisted, surpassed all of that.

That's why, on Dippy's walls, you saw Styx, Genesis, and Journey. There were large glossy pictures of The Who, The Grateful Dead, as well as Queen. More posters show-

cased Rolling Stones, Rush, and The Doors. Rounding out
the group was Black Sabbath, Moody Blues, and Nirvana.

Denny caught me looking around.

"That's you," He pointed to the poster area.

"What's me? Oh, you mean the Kurt thing?" I didn't
recall telling him about my suicide call.

"Huh? No. Look." Dippy pointed at one poster to another, deliberately.

I tried my best to follow.

"Breaking it down, Pipe. You're like the Queen, okay?
And you morph into this Rolling Stone, in a Rush, on a
Journey, through the Doors to Styx—because you died.
Your Moody Blues showed you Genesis, on that Black
Sabbath, when your heart stopped, and met The Who—
that guy, whatever his name is. You wanted to come out
of it being The Grateful Dead, but now you can only hope
to achieve Nirvana." Dippy was lit up with happiness; he
secured this marvelous new discovery about how my life
was written in posters.

"You're so high." I couldn't help but laugh.

"I'm not." Dippy crossed his arms over his chest.

"No, no, no." I smiled at him. "Don't take it the wrong
way. This is way cool, honestly. You have, like, a profound
way of putting things in perspective, complete with cool
props." I grinned at Dippy, moved my palm to his cheek,
and gently tapped it. "You're all right, Corporal Marino.
First class kind of guy, you know?"

"You're such a bullshitter."

"Yeah. And?"

"And..." Dippy's voice trailed off.

I knew something was wrong; however, I also knew it could potentially trigger an intense PTSD attack, and I didn't want that to happen, so I had to try to get him out of it. But he spoke first.

"Piper."

"Dip."

"I have to tell you something."

"Oh God, what?" I groaned. Don't tell me you pulled an Oedipus and slept with Mom."

"What? Jesus, no. Why do you say such weird things?" Dippy shuddered, and contorted his visage into disgust—like when you've just taken a bite of some bread, and realized how there's mold caked on the bottom. "But, anyway... Arella from the hospital..."

I brought Arella to the forefront of my mind. I thought she was going to be a magnificent caretaker, but she turned out to be strange, and made me feel uncomfortable. I still had no idea what her purpose was, and figured I would do some sort of Internet search on it when I got back up to my bedroom. However, I remained there so Dippy could tell his story.

"Back in Iraq, I was scared shitless on a constant basis. But not as scared shitless as I feel right now, do you know what I mean?" He nervously scratched at his collar. "I had my comrades, there. Yeah, it sucked, but I was able to grin and bear it because… because I was in a different sort of shit. Look at me now: I don't have my leg, anymore. My fucking family is falling apart. Piper, you tried to fucking kill yourself. I don't know what's going on in Abigail's head. She's so young, and she tries so hard to be older. Dad is always working—or says he's always working. I mean, who knows anymore, is my point. Either way, he's home by midnight, and out the door again by dawn. Mom is probably going to die of cancer sometime in the next ten years because of her chain-smoking, and you'll get stuck being a mom to Abby. And, Christ, I never wanted that life for you. Ever. This isn't the way things were supposed to pan out. They promised me the fucking world. Promised I'd have everything I'd ever want, or need, when I got back home. With honor."

He pushed the pot away from him. I knew Dippy wanted me to see how sober he was, or tried to be, when he said what he had to say. I hated seeing him so serious, frightened, and on the verge of tears. Before he enlisted, I only saw my brother cry maybe once or twice.

"In Iraq," he continued. "When I stepped on the goddamn IED in the ground, I was mad at myself like you couldn't imagine. It was so careless on my part. Wasn't like insurgents attacked us directly. But it blew my leg right off, and I passed out. Couldn't take the pain, or the blood, or I don't know. But I went right down, and I lost consciousness. And I had this dream. You're not gonna believe me, Pipe, but just hear me out."

Dippy was shaking. It wasn't a rare occurrence. He was so skinny, and pale, that he couldn't help but feel cold all the time. Not to mention how he always wore boxers at home, and little else. Dippy was bull-headed.

"Anyway." Dippy moved the pizza box aside, since we were done eating, and lay back on the mattress, next to me, and kept his eyes focused on the ceiling, as if he could see his thoughts played out on it. "I traveled through this bright beam of light, you know? It wasn't darkness. Now, I don't know if it was one of those died-and-came-back experiences, like maybe you had. Who knows? But, still, I was floating up there, and still had my leg attached. I landed on this, like, cloud type of thing. It was solid, though. Around me, it was bright, bright, bright. Almost blinding, but it didn't hurt my eyes. The first thing I saw after the clouds, right, was this woman walking toward me. That Arella woman from the hospital, I swear."

Goose bumps covered my skin.

Dippy shook again, and my eyes became gigantic dishes. Unsure of what to do, exactly, I grabbed a blanket, wrapped it around him and draped my arm across his shoulders.

"Did she say anything to you?"

"Well. She was like, 'Dennis, boy, why in the world would you enlist in that war?'" Dippy smiled the same bashful smile that he flashed at Arella in the hospital.

"And then what?"

"And then I was like, 'I don't know, anymore. I thought I knew.' And she said, 'Of course you don't know. No one knows.'" Dippy concluded with a shrug.

I scratched at my head again. A small scab was forming, so I moved my hands away and pressed them palm-side-down against the mattress.

"Do you think it's just some weird kind of coincidence, Dip?"

"No." He shook his head. "Not at all."

"Oh come on, Dip, do you really believe in shit like that?"

"I do now," he confirmed. "She was right, though. There's no real reason to sign up beyond the smoke and mirrors. Pipe dreams, right? I mean, yeah, you're promised things like money and education, except they never fucking tell you that you have to take, and pass, all of these exams, and shit like that. And I never passed, Pipe. Never."

"But you're so smart." I decided to drop the Arella issue.

"I lost a lot of what was in here." He gestured to his head. "A whole lot. Add to the fact that I have trouble with my thoughts, always shifting, shifting, shifting. I never got anything they promised. And Grandma paid for half of the prosthetic."

"Geez, Dip." I gaped at him with pure amazement. No

one had ever told me any of those facts, because no one ever knew except Denny. And he didn't talk about the war, ever, so I was shocked that he decided to spill what he had inside of him. It was probably a part of his catharsis.

"I was too gullible."

"Yeah, but," I interjected. "You joined because you wanted to defend the country, right?"

"Honestly, Pipe." Dippy shook his head. "I did it mostly just to get the fuck away from here. Home, I mean. You remember what it was like between us. But I regretted it right after that picture of us was taken." He glanced over at the framed photograph. "As soon as I got on the plane, I cried the entire way there. I never cried like that in my life."

I was floored.

Dippy had always been one of those I-Love-America people. He shouted the usual slogans of backwards morons, like, "Love it or leave it!" and "Land of the free, home of the brave!" He tacked the American flag over his bed, and thoughtfully mulled over politics, like which political party would be right for him. Eventually he settled on the GOP, like our mother. I never took a liking to politics, and, instead, registered as an Independent. Dad was fiercely Democratic, though, and he and Dippy would argue often, and loudly, at the dinner table.

The problem with Dippy's newfound love for America post-attack, was he became a scathing asshole about certain issues. Dippy's Confederate flag t-shirt was worn with pride, despite Dad and me feeling pure disgust.

"We're not even from the goddamn South," I had bitched at a younger, muscled, confident Dippy. It was just a few months after the attack on .

"It's just about what it represents," he'd retorted.

"Oh, yeah? And what's that?"

"You're not from Italy, but what kind of flag is hanging above your bed? Oh, right, a fucking Italian one!"

"It's the Italy National Soccer Team, asshole! Answer my question."

"It represents–"

"I'll tell you what it represents: it fucking represents hatred for *us* northerners—you know, us *Yankees*, and it's a symbol of hate in general. Black people hate it because, you know, remember the whole slavery thing? Yeah. That. And Jews hate it, too. Neo-Nazis and the KKK use their stupid flag during their shitty little cross-burning sessions." I had been infuriated; my fists were clenched into balls, my cheeks flushed a deep magenta, and my eyes were narrowed.

"It represents being proud of being white. And there's nothing wrong with that!"

"In your context, it is!"

"At least I don't support terrorism," he'd seethed.

"Prajin is Indian, and a Hindu. He has nothing to do with terrorism and he *does not poison his bagels*!" I had been on the verge of hitting my brother; it didn't matter that he had a significant height and weight advantage. Neither of us ever wanted to acquiesce.

Now, years later, Dippy was not the same man. He had grown up after going through the horrors of war. The shirt became an embarrassment to him, and so did his past life.

"SEEING HER THERE, IT was like the weirdest thing ever. Same hair, nose, eyes. The same manner of speaking. Nothing changed. I tried to shrug it off or something, but now I can't stop thinking about it." Dippy shook his head, and buried his face in his hands. He was still shaking.

I stretched my arm and plucked an Oxy from the stem of his drug flower. Dippy, hearing my movement, tucked his hands under his head and opened his mouth.

"You are such a fucking pill popper," I teased.

"Give me a break." Dippy groaned. "I've got one leg!"

"Better than no legs." I dropped the green relief into his mouth. He swallowed and licked his lips with his pierced tongue.

"Hey, Pipe?"

"Hm?"

"How come you didn't come down and steal all of my stash if you wanted to kill yourself?"

It was a legitimate question, I knew. I never thought he would actually ask me, though, so I was caught off-guard.

"Um, well. I just, you know, I guess that like, it would have been super fucked up of me to take a whole bunch of pills from my brother who's a, like, amputee veteran and lives in constant pain. You know, psychologically, emotionally, and physically."

Dippy rolled his eyes at me and threw a Xanax in my direction. I caught it. "You're depressed as fuck," he declared. "Have a benzo."

"Nah, I'm just…" I trailed off, unsure of what I was, exactly.

"Depressed. Really fucking depressed. You have to be in order to try and take your own life."

"Mom's depressed." I wrinkled my nose. "I'm just stupid."

"You're not stupid. You're really fucking smart, which is why I still can't believe you did what you did. You know that Mom and Dad are dragging you to a shrink, right? To, like, get your life back on track, or whatever phrase."

"No," I protested. "No fucking way. I don't want to go."

"I mean, Pipe, you tried to lightning yourself to death."

"I had reasons."

"Crazy ones."

"Legitimate."

"Legitimately crazy."

"Serious reasons!"

"Come on," he groaned. "None of all of what you told is enough to fucking off yourself. I think it's probably the best idea to go and get yourself some psychiatric help."

"A lot of good it did you," I snapped. I knew I shouldn't have said the words as soon as they left my mouth.

"I'm alive. You almost didn't make it to twenty-three."

"Neither did you."

"For different reasons."

"Oh, yeah?"

We stared at each other. Around me, the air hummed. My head was light, and I wished that my brother and I had never gotten into an argument. It was becoming a buzzkill for the both of us. What was supposed to be a relaxed evening with my favorite sibling deviated into yet another round of bullshit. I thought back to the fight we had years ago; it had ended with me shoving Denny until he'd lost balance and hit his head on the kitchen cabinet. He had chased me around the house, trying to sweep my legs, but I'd run out the back door, up the hill to the shopping center, and bought two dozen bagels.

"Okay; we're the same kind of fuck up," Dippy said. "Only at least I wanted to actually help people. America."

I got up after Dippy's last word, and popped the Xanax into my mouth, swallowing it dry.

"You know," I said. "Don't think I don't remember the time you tried to fucking kill yourself, too. Except Mom fucking found you on the floor, having a seizure from your overdose, and we rushed you to the hospital. But no one talks about the incident, because you're fucked up from the war. And my problems can never be as serious as that!" I folded my arms across my chest and huffed.

"Drama, drama, drama." Dippy leaned back on his hands. "Life isn't as crappy as you think it is. And my overdose was an accident, okay? I just forgot how much I had taken, and then I took too much, and that's the story."

"Bullshit," I hissed.

"I don't have a death wish. I'm not you!"

I marched up to my bedroom, leaving my one-legged brother to enjoy his pot and pills.

Dippy was always more than capable of doing or saying something to piss me off, but he hadn't done anything aggravating since he returned home. I wasn't sure what to do; part of me wanted to stay, cry, hug him, and apologize. But the pissed off part took over, and I was gone.

8

Damaged

THE PILL HIT ME when I got to my bathroom. Along the way, I passed my arguing parents. Mom was sobbing, and Dad had his hand firmly gripped on her shoulder. For sure, I didn't want to get in the middle of whatever was going on. Arguing, making up, negotiating; it was best to avoid all of it, and just wish for the best. They had their fights from time to time, but Mom never told Dad that she wanted a separation. It was taboo in our family. It was probably something that should have been done a long time ago, but they had both put up with each other for the sake of us, their religion, and their cultures. I never thought my parents were a satisfactory match. Dad was free-spirited, enjoyed laughing, and never crossed a picket line. Mom, on the other hand, was stiff, insecure, and more stubborn than the rest of the clan combined. They say how opposites attract, but they don't give a time-line.

In the bathroom, I took a long glance at myself in the mirror. I was a mess. My eyes were red from either the pot, stress, or the buildup of the salty stuff in my ducts; because I was stressed out and tired, puffy purple curtains hung under my eyes. I was a zombie, but at least my hair was clean. For sure, I reeked of pot, so I spritzed on some perfume to cover the stench, and I found my way into my bedroom.

Once inside, I hopped onto my bed and glanced around. My personal effects were still completely intact, which amazed me. What if they never found any of my suicide stuff? It was careless of me to not leave a gigantic neon arrow pointing at it. Maybe a flashing sign would have been ideal. The flag above my bed reminded me of the soccer game coming up—the one I wasn't going to—and gloom set in.

I picked up my cell phone. It had been fully charged before I went out on the balcony to die, but now it only had one battery bar left. There were no text messages, missed phone calls, or voicemails. The battery color switched to red. I dialed anyway.

"This is the Suicide Hotline," a concerned-sounding

woman stated.

Shit.

"Hey, um, hi. Is Jerry around?"

"Jerry...who?"

"I don't know his last name. Just... Jerry."

"Miss, if this is a prank call..."

"No, no. It isn't. I swear. I spoke to Jerry a few days ago is all, and I would like to speak to him again this time, you know? It's my suicide comfort zone and all."

The other end of the line was silent for a moment.

"Hold, please."

I had no idea how the hotline worked, but I wanted to hear the last voice I heard before I stepped out onto the balcony. I chewed on my bottom lip, and moved from my bed, to my chair, though it was impossible to sit still. I played with the ends of my hair and listened to the music in the background. It was some muzak version of an unidentified song, probably from the eighties, though the early nineties sounded a whole lot like the late eighties as far as pop was concerned. At least that's what my mom told me.

"Suicide Hotline," the gruff, tired-sounding voice said.

"Jerry!" I yelled.

"Yes? This is Jerry." He sounded a bit confused, but who could blame him?

"It's me, Piper. Do you remember me?"

"Piper? Oh! Yes. Of course I remember you. You

pulled through."

"I almost didn't, Jerry," I confessed. I quickly launched into what had happened in the past few days. If Jerry actually caught any of the babbling, I had no idea. I knew it was sort of wrong of me to tie up the lines, but I believed my situation was important enough to eat away some time. Maybe the glittering moment of reverie I had was just that: a moment. There was no guarantee things were going to get any better. Denny's issues were probably too crippling for him to ever move on, and out of the basement.

Because my folks were probably splitting up, Dad could go live the bachelor lifestyle that he probably needed. Denny could blaze up until his posters played music and moved around. All Mom ever wanted was Abigail, and now she could have her. Everything *would* work out if I did it—no third wheel syndrome. Shit, we didn't even have a cat or dog around to keep me company, and the television and Internet could only do so much. New Zealand felt farther away than it ever had.

Jerry was silent as I explained everything to him—the lightning, the nurse-angels, and the weird dream about Lucian. And I explained about my parents' upcoming separation, and my feelings about how I still wasn't convinced that living was the right choice.

"I think, maybe, I want to get it right this time, Jerry," I explained. "No more mess ups. Actual death. The reset button."

"Piper, listen. You mentioned about having some sort of a plan, now. You have money for school and you *can* move in with your dad and brother soon, right? As long as you give it a legitimate try? Feeling desperate is something that happens to all of us, and I know that you're seeing the glass half-empty right now, but mull over the potential positives. So there are very important things to look forward to. Life isn't all doom-and-gloom. It is what we make it."

Jerry was sort of right, I guessed, but why delay the inevitable, anyway?

"Well, about the plan... weighing the pros and cons here, Dad's probably going to need money to fork over to Mom for my sister's school when she gets full custody and makes him pay out of the ass for all the expenses. And my brother? I don't know. We just had a fight. As optimistic as I want to be about him, I don't think he's ever going to get any better. And I know that sounds all kinds of wrong, and cynical, and horrible, but I mean, why deny the truth? He's so damaged. We're all so damaged. There just aren't enough Band-Aids to stick over us."

"There are so many years ahead to right the wrongs. You have a family, and I know they love you. And you love them, too."

"Maybe I just don't want to be me, anymore."

"Piper, what can I do to talk you out of this?"

"I don't know, Jerry. Want to give me a new life? How does that sound? I can live with you. Cook, clean, do laundry. But I suck at sweeping."

"That's ah, flattering, Piper. Except I'm married."

"Kids?"

"Two."

"Well, congratulations."

"Thanks. And we all like the same ice cream flavor: rocky road."

I couldn't help but laugh. "I pegged you as a vanilla guy, to be honest. Sugar cone."

"In my younger years, maybe. Now it's all about rocky road. In a waffle cone."

"I haven't had one of those in years."

"Maybe you should."

"You're a great guy, Jerry. Take care of yourself, okay? Thanks for being there for me."

"Piper, I have to tell you something—"

My cell phone died in the palm of my hand. The soft tinkling music sounded, and then it was gone. I stuck the charger into it, and tossed it on my desk. Jerry's positive outlook, though sweet, was not enough to yank me out of my slump. I thought about back at the hospital, the awful sinking feeling when I realized that I wasn't dead. And I thought about how my family was so torn up to see me there, in the hospital bed, a victim of my own mind.

I was glad, at least, that I wasn't constantly being

watched by my family. They were all too focused on what they were doing, anyway. Dippy was probably fast asleep from his drugs, Mom and Dad were dealing with their issues in the kitchen, and the little pageant munchkin was getting a lesson in rainbow kisses from her stupid friend. She would be home in a short time, I estimated, since there was no way she would be allowed to sleep over again the night before a major holiday. Abigail still believed in the Easter Bunny, and my mother insisted we let her relish in her vivid imagination. I discovered the truth about the Bunny when I was a few years younger than Abigail. The Tooth Fairy's tale came to an end before that, but Santa lived on until I was seven. I used to think, sometimes, how maybe God was a myth, too, and instead of giving people money, or gifts, he only chose a select few, while other people got cancer and poverty.

"Fuck it." I stepped out onto the balcony.

The sky was a blotch of dark navy ink, sprinkled with flecks of glowing stars. They reminded me of the stars in my dream. With Lucian. A gentle breeze swayed around me, making me shiver, since my hair was still damp. I wrapped my arms around myself. My thoughts wandering back to the night prior. It felt as though years had passed. I glanced at the rows of backyards facing my balcony. Some people had their bedroom lights on, but no one was outside enjoying the evening.

The baseball bat lay on the floor.

"Okay." I glanced upward at the sky. "You win this round, Jerry. I'll go back inside."

A hand grasped my shoulder and I jumped, my breath hitched in my throat.

"What the fuck, Denny!"

"I told you," a deep voice growled into my ear. "The game is on."

"Jesus Christ!" I shrieked.

"Not quite."

9

Filius Diabolus

H E WAS STILL THE same, facially; though, this time he was in an all-black suit, with the first few buttons on the shirt undone. I didn't know if this was a hallucination from the pot and Xanax, if I fell asleep and was now dreaming, if I lost my mind, or of this was real. Any of the possibilities were plausible at that moment.

"What do you mean the game is on?" I hissed. I was not backing down from him. If it was real, or a dream, I had nothing to lose. I was desperate and on the verge of a nervous breakdown. Unless that was what it all was.

"I mean, we continue. You remember where we last left off, don't you?" His eyes slowly meandered from mine down to my scar, though he offered no apologetic gesture. In fact, he was pleased. It was the polar reaction I was previously given, though I didn't like either one.

I narrowed my eyes, still unable to tell reality from fantasy.

"Who *are* you?" I wondered.

"Are we going to have to go through this each time? I'm Lucian."

"Okay, I know who you are but *what* are you?"

"Now that," he pointedly said, "is the question you should have asked me first."

Lucian was nothing but confident. I, on the other hand, was ready to start screaming like a little girl for my dad. I wondered if he, too, could see the man on the balcony. I had the distinct feeling Lucian could have overpowered me in a nanosecond if it was real. And then what—my dad would come running, and be met with certain doom? I wasn't going to put his life in danger, and I didn't want any of them thinking how I was even crazier than they thought.

"Okay, so pretend I asked it first."

"How very clever of you."

"Come on."

"*Filius Diabolus.*"

"The—"

"The Devil's son. But call me Lucian. I insist."

The son of the Devil? I didn't even know the Devil had

a son. God had a son, sure; it was pounded into my head for years and years during religious education classes with old lady Hennessey. But the son of the Devil? I had never heard of it before. I never much believed in the Devil to begin with, but part of me supposed, for every negative or positive, there had to be an equal opposite. God gets the Devil, Jesus gets... well he gets the Devil's son, apparently.

"Is Lucian your real name?"

"No."

"So what's your real name, Son of the Devil?"

"It isn't important; and, anyway, you wouldn't understand the language."

"I didn't know the Devil had a son."

"There are a few of us." He frowned and moved his stare to the baseball bat. My guard went up instinctively; I wanted to reach for it, but thought the better of the situation.

"Did I say something wrong?" I wondered.

"No."

"Are you the man in charge?"

"Something like that."

"You know, I don't know if you're real, or a figment of my imagination, but I'm tired, and I just don't want to deal with this right now. You're either a hallucination, or this is a dream, or, shit, maybe you are real. But, anymore, I just don't know. And my energy is draining." For sure, I knew it was ballsy of me to speak to him that way. Regardless of whether or not he was Lucifer's spawn, he was sizable, and muscular, and could have pummeled me into oblivion. If he was real. I edged closer to the rail on my balcony and held on tightly.

"What? Do you want a demonstration?"

I mulled the thought over for a moment. If I responded yes, and he was the real deal, something awful would happen. If I responded no, it meant I would be backing down, and he would have something over me. If I answered yes, and he wasn't capable of doing anything, I'd know he was just a crazy guy who managed to sneak into my house. And my dreams.

"Can it be a peaceful demonstration?" I inquired.

"Those are the worst kind," Lucian drawled. "I don't do parlor tricks. It isn't my forte."

"I bet." I wiped out the idea in my mind of challenging him to make an elephant appear out of, and disappear into, thin air.

Lucian removed a pair of dice from his pants pocket. They were metallic red, with black lacquer dots painted on them.

"Something simple. Please," I begged.

"If I roll anything other than a six, your sister is joyful and healthy. I roll a six, she will call in the preceding six seconds to tell your mom about how she feels nauseous. On the way home, she'll puke in your mother's car. Win-win. Don't lie to me and tell me you feel genuine love and affection for them. They're your rivals." His voice, deep and smooth, licked every word. It amazed me just how full of confidence he was. He spoke slowly and eloquently, with a rich deepness to his tone, as well as well as a dark type of gruffness. With certain words, Lucian reduced his volume to just a whisper. He obviously wanted me to feel enchanted by him, to cling to his every syllable. What he had to say about Mom and Abby was, essentially, correct. I disliked them both, though I did still love them out of familial obligation.

"Roll them," I declared. I knew where the dice would fall.

Lucian smirked, placed the dice in his gigantic palm, and held them up to my lips. "Blow."

Pursing my lips, I glanced up into his eyes; his pupils were dancing with delight. So I blew.

He enclosed his fingers around his palm and shuffled. The dice, red and glittering, bounced once, twice, three times on the floor of the balcony.

"Double threes. If my math is correct—which it always is—equals six."

"Maybe I do believe you. But maybe I don't. Abby's due home anyway, and–"

Ring.

Lucian smirked. I bit down on my lip and quietly walked back into my bedroom to pick up the line. I pressed the 'hold' button immediately, and I listened in on the conversation—Abigail was feeling ill. My mother was on her way.

I hung up and spun around, only to see Lucian sitting on my bed.

"Did you really need dice for that?"

"They add flair," he smirked.

"Parlor—"

"You've never had a man in here," he bluntly stated. "Family doesn't count."

"Um, no. I guess I haven't. How do you know?"

"I know everything about you." Lucian smirked at me. It made my hands all clammy, and there was a sudden tightness around my neck. I wasn't sure what he was trying to get at, but I didn't think I was going to like it. "Including your virgin soul," he growled. "So very rare that we get one these days. But you…"

"Personal business!"

"Nothing about you is personal business, anymore."

Lucian's eyes darted to my chest. My heart. My scar.

"You were marked," he stated. He casually lounged on my bed, his feet sticking out from the bottom, because he was far too tall for it.

"From the lightning, yeah," I explained. "Got this weird, like, upside-down question mark scar from it. Dip—Denny's dog tags must've—"

"It wasn't the metal from the tags."

"Then what?"

He got up from the bed, and was immediately in front of me. I looked up to meet his stare. His breathing was even, but the air coming out of him was fire. It was a stark contrast to my own cold breath, though being near him certainly warmed me a few degrees.

Lucian placed his hand over my heart, and I shuddered. It was uncomfortable, like the first time he had done so—in the dream.

"I don't like it when you do that," I explained. I attempted to squirm away from him, but Lucian didn't let me.

"The upside-down question mark, as you so crassly call it, is the mark of *Ego Interfectum*; self-murder. We call it *Animam Edere,* meaning to give up your spirit. It was exactly what you did when you decided to go through with the suicide, except you tricked me and got me into this whole mess."

"No, I didn't."

"Oh, you most certainly did."

"I don't even know what you're talking about." I was exasperated, on the verge of tears. I didn't realize how ordinary my life had been just two days prior.

"You were brought back to this life, even though you and I were about to have a very nice time together." He flicked his eyes to me, and, slowly, moved them along the length of my body, stopping, again, at where the scar was. It was making me even more self-conscious than usual.

"I don't remember any of it."

"You could." He sat up on the bed. "If you want to agree to my..."

"Terms and conditions?"

"That's an acceptable phrase."

Against my better judgment, I seated myself opposite of the Devil's son. He was right—it was the first time a man had been in my bedroom—and on my bed, no less.

This is not the way I had imagined it. I could have had a boyfriend, once, during my first semester of college. In high school, I'd paid no attention to anything other than my studies, music, and family. Friends had been scarce, even back in those days. I'd always been a loner. My parents called it my middle-child syndrome, but it was just who I was. In college, though, I had met a terrific guy in my Astronomy class. He and I had sat next to each other, but I was too shy to say much beyond asking him for a spare sheet of paper, or to shuffle through his notes, or to borrow a pen. He'd made me laugh when he made cracks about the professor, and I'd always hoped, maybe, he would ask to get to know me outside of room two-twenty-seven, but he didn't. When the end of the semester rolled around, he'd told me how he was going to miss sitting next to me. Instead of pouring my feelings out, I had awkwardly jerked my shoulders and muttered about how, yeah, I'd need to find someone else to borrow pens from.

BRINGING ME BACK TO the present, Lucian cocked his head to the side, and stared at me once more.

"Still doubting my existence? You know what's about to happen with these family members of yours."

I did know. Abigail was on her way home with Mom, and they would both seclude themselves in the master bedroom. Dippy would be out cold for a few hours from all of the pills he was going to consume, and Dad would probably leave the house, opting to find solace somewhere entirely different—it could have been something innocent like a buddy's house for a game of cards, or go the lake for some late-night fishing. There was the possibility he would go to a bar or a strip club, too. And who could blame him? Poor Dad, he didn't receive much of any affection from Mom, as she was too busy making sure Abigail was going to be privileged and proper, giving the little brat what none of us ever had.

Mom would always say how it was a mistake to have fallen in love with Dad, because Dad didn't make a lot of money. She would tell Abigail, despite her age, to go after the multi-millionaires. Or, better yet, the billionaires.

"I'd rather have money than love," Mom always used to say.

"I'd rather have your love than all of the money in the world," Dad would reply.

"Bruno," Mom would grunt, "You are so full of shit."

"Not everyone is so materialistic." I'd chime in. "Luckily your gene didn't get thrown into my mix. That would've been a fucking plague, let me tell you."

"Piper," Mom would interject. "Mind your own fucking business, for once."

"Enough," Dad would bark. "She's got the right to speak up in here."

Those were Sunday dinner conversations.

Every ten minutes or so, Abigail would say something stupid: I put sixteen grapes in my mouth; Diamonds are a girl's best friend; Piper, your shoes are ugly.

I BLINKED.

Lucian was inching closer to me, sinister as ever.

"By the way, your dad went to the bar, downtown. Apparently, he needed to get away from, *quote*, all of this insanity, *unquote*. Don't worry, he'll be safe. He isn't the reason why I'm here. Even your moron brother, who failed at *Ego Interfectum*, isn't on my agenda for now. So would you like to venture a guess as to who I'm here for?"

"You mean... you're taking me away with you?"

"I would not have come all this way just to—what do you mortals say—borrow a cup of sugar. Oh, and don't worry. No one is coming to check on you. So much concern for Piper."

Panic ran through me. My legs, once normal and capable of doing things like walking and running, were reduced to Jell-O. Both of my arms went numb, though I wasn't sure if it was due to paralyzing fear, or the onset of a heart attack. Either way, I was terrified.

Lucian watched me in genuine amusement. He was sitting on my computer chair, slowly swiveling it around to his liking.

"The trip down may make you dizzy. I suggest drinking water. The hydration will come in handy, given the warmth of the atmosphere."

On the bed, I was hyperventilating. I shoved myself off of it, and fell down onto the floor, where my cheek pressed firmly against the cold hardwood. It was refreshing to have my body cool down. My blood pressure must have rocketed up to Mars. Lucian didn't bother checking to see if I was okay—and why would he, anyway? If I died on the spot, he could do whatever he wanted with my soul.

Lucian handed me a bottle of water from my mini-refrigerator. It amazed me how he could show an act of kindness as all of this was going on. He was inherently evil after all, wasn't he? Though it seemed taboo to ask, I wanted to bombard him with all sorts of questions. Sure, it was just a shame that all he wanted to do with me is take my soul and be on his way. It wasn't like I knew the process or anything. I had been willing to give up my life, but the best possible chance I had was in Hell. I would never get to see Heaven because of my suicide. It terrified me. I regretted not speaking to the angels longer. They might have been able to help. But now I was stuck. I wondered about Arella and Hael, and if they were what they claimed to be. They must have been livid with me for brushing them off. I would have been, too. To them, I was nothing more than a brat who refused help; I chose the path, and had to follow it. There was no other way, not with Lucian ready to whisk me away to his hometown.

I drank deeply from the plastic bottle, not caring how the contents were spilling down, drenching me in the process—my mouth, cheeks, shirt, arms, hands, and some on the legs. I was never neat.

I thought a silent prayer when I had the breather:
Our Father, who art in heaven,
Hallowed be thy name;
Thy kingdom come, thy will be done-

"NOW, PIPER." LUCIAN SAW I had calmed down. "Let me explain what's about to happen."

I peered at the six-foot-four walking muscle, and cringed. Lucian hovered over me; and, when I glanced up from the floor, I could see he had rolled his eyes at me. Yes, I certainly was a pathetic mess. I managed to roll over onto my back, still breathing heavily, and finished the rest of the water.

He snarled. "It's like watching a child. Humans. Entirely incapable of getting anything right."

I was far beyond the point of exhaustion. "What are

the terms?"

"Thank you for asking, Piper."

Under normal circumstances, I usually always respond to politeness with a smile. This was not a normal circumstance.

"I want your soul, because I've earned it. You surrendered it. *Animam Edere.* So let's negotiate, to make this easier. What do you want with the limited time you have left?" He surveyed me with interest. I was waiting for him to take out a paper and pen for my list of demands, but he had none. Probably did it internally. He sat down beside me, and pulled me into a sitting position. My lips went numb.

"Well." I paused for a moment to think. "For starters, I want you to show me what happened when I died. Where I was taken, and what I did. You mentioned how I went back. I want it all shown to me. Explained. Dissected."

"Anything else?"

"My family. Don't fuck with them. Just leave them alone, okay? They've done nothing that concerns you." I folded my arms over my chest. It was juvenile, sure, but it always worked on my dad when I wanted something he was on the fence about purchasing.

"You do realize," Lucian continued. "If I agree to your stipulations, I will be collecting your soul. You'll die, the way you wanted to. The way it should have been. And life, to these mortals, will resume. They will mourn you, yes, but they will get over it and move on with their lives, in time."

I pictured Lucian as a bounty hunter—the bounties being souls. He would jump into a Humvee, or something otherwise gigantic and environmentally unnecessary, and chase down the intact souls, suck them through some elaborate machine, and be a hero to the Underworld.

I laughed.

"What in the world are you laughing about?"

"Oh. No. Nothing. But what happens to my soul? You know? I mean, do I go in some type of jar somewhere and sit on a shelf for eternity? Is it like Dante—do I get thrown into, you know, circle seven and stuff? The ones who do violence against themselves. Suicides, you know, they inhabit the second ring, which Dante called a horrid forest. Awful, isn't it? It's not what I want." I bit down on my lip.

"This isn't Dante's *Inferno*." His fists clenched.

"Well, it's my frame of reference."

"I was sent to collect you. I'm through waiting around. I agree to your requests."

My head spun. "Do we shake hands?"

Lucian shook his head.

"Prepare," he warned. "For eternity, and brace for impact." Lucian lowered his arm and grabbed hold of mine, but he screamed and recoiled.

"Holy Water!" he roared.

I could see Lucian's skin bubble up, and it was rendered bloodred, and swelled with pus. It was disgusting. Wherever he touched the water, he was immediately affected by it. I had no idea why nobody heard the ruckus and came running, but it was probably better for all of them, anyway.

"Shit!" I yelled. I wildly wrung my hands. I didn't want to piss off the son of Satan. "I honestly had no idea. I didn't mean to. I mean, I swear. I swear I didn't mean to do it, Lucian. I didn't even know. It was just drinking water. I must... I... I had been thinking is all."

"Thinking about *what*?"

"The, um, The Lord's Prayer."

Lucian glared at me incredulously. Mostly, it looked like he wanted to rip my head off and eat it. Sweat was forming on his bronzed body, his eyes were blazing blue, and his teeth were bared. Lucian's nostrils were flared. A bull about to charge.

"Next time," Lucian muttered. "After I get this sorted out, we're leaving."

Lucian walked out onto the balcony.

"Lucian?"

"*What*, human?"

"Will it be tomorrow?"

He shook his head. His body appeared to be tight and edgy; clenching, unclenching, and once again clenching various body parts.

"No."

"Why not?"

"We cannot…"

"Because of Easter?"

He scowled, and disappeared after a few steps.

I stared at the spot, wondering what could possibly happen next. Below me, I heard my mother's car pull up onto the driveway. A few moments later, Abigail's whine filled the night air. Her tummy hurt, she complained. Mine did, too.

10

Easter

I WAS AWAKENED EASTER morning by a loud screeching coming from my sister's bedroom. No one reacted.

"Mom!" Abby screamed. "Mom! Mom! Mom!"

"Jesus *H*. Christ," my mom answered from downstairs. "What is it, Abigail? Are you hurt?"

"No!" she called back.

"What the fuck is wrong with you?" My eyes adjusted to the light when I walked into her bedroom. It was princess-themed; an explosion of bubblegum-pink, with frills, glitter, and rhinestones. Abby, dressed in her fuzzy bunny nightgown, with matching fuzzy bunny slippers, let out a heavy sob. She wiped her snotty nose on her sleeve, hiccupped, and sobbed once more.

"I didn't get anything from the Easter Bunny!"

Downstairs, my mother stopped rustling her papers. The silence lasted a moment.

"Hey, Abby…" I glanced down at my sister. I would have normally told her the stupid Easter Bunny wasn't real; how it was just some bullshit fairytale that chocolate companies exploited to make millions of dollars. I didn't tell her she was too old to still believe in such stupid, fictional nonsense. I didn't tell her any of it, because, if someone told it to me about Lucian, I would have told them they were dead wrong.

Abby peered up at me. Her doll-blue eyes were brimming with tears.

"Let me tell you what I asked the Easter Bunny to do for you this year."

My mother appeared at the staircase; she and Abigail appeared intrigued. At least intrigued enough to not settle for such a shitty Easter morning, because she, even in her infinite brattiness, deserved more.

"Tell me," she pleaded.

"Okay. Well. I wrote a letter to the Easter Bunny and said he should make you go on an egg hunt, which will lead you to your treasure." I had to improvise. My sister eagerly hopped foot-to-foot. "He e-mailed me—we go a long ways back—and said he would. He also sent me instructions. So Mom is going to take you to do your first task, which is to get your Easter outfit on. And then you have to do your hair and, um, paint yourself up like a bunny."

"Wow!" Abigail was totally buying my lie.

"I'll be right here the whole time waiting!" I exclaimed.

"All right!"

I dashed into the house and grabbed hold of my dad, who was getting English muffin crumbs all over the comics. "Fuck!" I quickly had to throw something together. "Okay, not much time. Dad, go... go grab the Easter basket on the dining room table and put all of those colored eggs inside."

Dad, bless him, asked no questions and, instead, ran right in and collected the eggs as I ripped up slips of pastel-colored papers. I jotted down a few bullshit instructions, and sealed up the eggs.

"What now?" Dad wondered.

"Now we put shit in the basket." I grinned. "Money! Put money in. And go collect from Dippy. And Mom's wallet... and go get the chemistry textbook on top of my dresser. There's some cash in there. Hurry, go!"

Despite glancing at me as though I were an alien, my father complied.

I ran outside into the backyard, my bare feet getting dampened by the dew on the blades of cool grass. I put the red egg down first, and continued placing the remaining six in the hiding spots I had assigned. Fourth grade science came in handy because I was able to recall ROY G. BIV; red, orange, yellow, green, blue, indigo, and violet. As soon as violet was secured, I glanced around and was completely relieved when my dad came running out with his basket of cash.

"Jesus!" I exclaimed. My eyes widened. "How much money did you collect?"

Dad rustled through the bills. "Hundred bucks," he proudly said.

"Jesus!"

"What?"

"It seems excessive. She's just a kid."

"But she had a traumatic experience."

"Oh, please. I once walked in on—"

"Piper!"

"All right, all right."

I took the basket from his hands and hid it in the top-secret location: Denny's old camping tent. I took to hiding out in it from time to time, when the world is at its worst. At least there was nothing incriminating inside. Once the basket was in, I zipped it up and ran back over to my Dad. He was just shy of optimistic.

Within minutes, Abigail was in full face paint as a bunny rabbit, and she bounded into the backyard in her damn pageant dress. She was grinning toothily, as though she had just been awarded Miss Congeniality—a title which would never be awarded to me. She was so perky and did not care about the state of the world. Things like poverty didn't concern her. Her whole world was what went on in the confines of our house, neighborhood, and town. Surely she wasn't connected to the city itself, because the isolation bubble did not extend that far out. She was just a kid, dressed up like a baby prostitute, waiting to play a game that would lead her to a prize: cold, hard cash. My little sister was going to be expecting chocolates and stuffed bunnies, but something told me she would like the monetary award far better. Meanwhile, the son of the Devil was after me.

"What is this?" Abigail screamed once her prize was discovered.

"Oh!" Mom squealed, snapping a picture with the digital camera. "A cash basket!"

"Hear those are the new big thing," Dennis chimed in. He had ventured out of the basement, half-dressed in an old pair of blue sweatpants. His prosthetic was on, and he had his pimp cane in hand.

"I don't want *this*," Abigail whined. She was grasping the fanned-out bills. "What am I going to do with *this*?"

"Buy... stuff," Dad suggested.

"I don't want to buy my own stuff." Abigail, in full tantrum-mode, stomped her foot down onto the ground. She also threw the cash up in the air. I quickly salvaged it, walking on my knees to pick up the last two bills. Poor honest Abe.

"This'll teach you some responsibility." It was obvious Dad wanted to get back to the newspaper, eat another English muffin, and not have to think about how all of his children had something incredibly wrong with them.

"I don't want responsibility as my prize! I'm just a kid!" Abby whined. She had managed to silence us. My dad surveyed his three kids: Abigail, me, and then Denny. He went back inside, either to stick his head in the oven, or to continue with his usual Sunday routine of perusing the newspaper.

"I'm sure Mom will take you to whatever store you want to go to, and you can get whatever you want," I commented.

"A chinchilla?"

"No," Mom insisted. "No way."

"This is the worst day ever." Abigail stomped her foot on the ground.

"No," Mom once again said. "I think Good Friday was the worst day ever."

"Agreed," said Dippy.

Without looking back at my family, I returned to my bedroom and crawled beneath my covers. Now that everything was upside-down, I just wanted darkness. Peaceful darkness. Nothing scary or euphoric. Our lives were filled with constant and consistent noise, whether we realized it or not. I slipped into unconsciousness in the blink of an eye.

DENNY WOKE ME UP. I pulled the covers off of my head and peeked at the clock. It read eleven fifty-nine. I was surprised I had slept the entire day away, more than sixteen hours, completely uninterrupted. I surveyed my chest; and, defeated, I was dealt yet another wave of misery when I discovered how my scar wasn't any better. I had put ointment on it, but it wasn't doing the trick.

"Hey, Pipe." Dippy beamed at me. "Delivery."

"There's only one minute left of Easter," I said, yawning.

"Well, you better get to eating, then." Denny had forced himself up the stairs with the use of his pimp cane, causing pride to swell up into my body. He was also wearing a backpack, so I knew where my food was coming from.

"Thanks for doing this for me, Dip."

"No problem." He dropped the cane onto the floor, and tossed the backpack onto my bed, where I snatched it up. I grabbed a Saint Joseph pastry. I took a bite and noted the time: one minute after midnight.

"So close," Dip said. He noticed where my eye-line was.

"Mhm," I nodded. I didn't care; the pastry, filled with rich cannoli cream, was too delicious.

Denny and I ate in silence for a few minutes. He

reeked of weed, so I knew he just wanted to enjoy the various explosions of flavors and textures from the leftovers. When he grabbed his Gatorade, I jumped on the chance to ask questions.

"Why didn't anyone wake me up?"

"Huh?"

"For dinner. Lamb. No one woke me up. What's that all about?"

"Oh." He wiped the red drink off his mouth. "Mom told us just let you sleep, since you needed the rest, and there'd be plenty of leftovers when you woke up. And Dad just wanted to eat. Abby's giving us the silent treatment because, *quote*, this family is just too weird, *unquote*."

"Right." I stifled a laugh when my brother lowered his "air quotes" fingers. "Well, whatever. It's no big deal. And it's true. Did you talk about me?"

"Nah." He stuffed a cannoli in his mouth, chewing like a cow.

"You so did."

"Nah."

"Come on, tell me."

"Just..." he sighed. "About your psychiatrist."

"Psychiatry is bullshit," I spat. "It's bullshit on top of bullshit, covered in fucking bullshit sauce. That's what psychiatry is. And I don't want to go."

"Jesus, Pipe, why don't you tell me how you really feel?"

I rolled my eyes at my brother. A gesture too harsh for what he said, though he did know my stance on the matter.

"You know. It just never worked for Mom."

"Yeah."

"Ten years."

"Some stuff worked."

"Not enough."

I wondered what my mother was doing. What she was thinking. I was desperate to know what was beyond the surface. Not what we all saw, the façade, but the actual raw emotion and feeling. That kind of honesty was incapable of being brought up to the surface when it came to my mother. There will always be too many things keeping the magma at bay; though, if there were to come a day when she exploded, I feared no one would be safe. Except Abigail.

What Abigail was doing was totally irrelevant to my thought process. She and I were square, as far as I was concerned. It was my best effort, and she would enjoy the cash basket sometime.

"We'll never be normal," I grumbled.

Denny frowned. "What's normal?"

"You know what I mean."

"I don't. Because normal doesn't exist. It never did. People just used to pretend better, is all."

Somewhere in the house my parents weren't pretending. Their marriage was disintegrating, and their family was going down a domino-line of destruction.

Denny messed my hair up.

"I'm going. You need sleep. Get ready to have your head shrunk."

"Happy fucking Easter to you, too."

11

The Shrink

DIPPY WAS RIGHT. AT eight o'clock on Monday morning, Dad roused me from my slumber by knocking hard on the bedroom door. After gorging on Easter food, I took two of the sleeping pills Dippy left on my nightstand.

I had been dreaming of Lucian, mostly just flashes and images, and didn't want to confront the day ahead of me.

"Pipe," Dad grunted on the other side of the door. "Get dressed and be downstairs in a few minutes. No time for a shower."

I sighed.

The night before, after gorging on pastries, I collapsed

onto my bed and curled up close to my pillow. It smelled like fabric softener—one of my favorite scents in the world. This particular one smelled of sweet lilacs and sunshine. Someone besides Mom had done the laundry. The smell, along with the soft tunes of classic piano CDs I owned, lulled me to sleep. I couldn't stand to sleep while wearing ear buds. I was a bit dated, sure, but it worked for me.

As I lay there, breathing in the comfort, my thoughts drifted to how warm Lucian's skin was. I had left my balcony doors ajar for cool air to infiltrate in, and I could not help but think how it would have been enjoyable to have him beside me, keeping me warm.

It was a sick thought, and I knew it. He wanted to take my soul away, and keep it with him, forever. Lucian was the epitome of evil; yet, I couldn't help but feel somewhat drawn to him. Perhaps if he was a hideous ogre, I could sort it out but, as it was, he was devilishly handsome.

Another rapping at my door caused me to jump up in bed.

"Piper!" my mother's harsh voice screeched. "Dressed and downstairs, *now*."

"I'm twenty-two for God's sake!"

After slipping out of bed, I caught my reflection in the mirror and winkled my nose. Staring back at me was a tired, disheveled mess, with an awful case of bed-head.

I wiggled out of the clothes I wore to bed, and stepped

into a pair of jeans. They were dark denim, and ripped at the knees. My mother attempted to repair them once, though it did not go well when I screamed. To complete the hot mess of an outfit, I tugged on a tank top, as well as a sweatshirt to go over it.

My hair, wild and long, got pulled back into a sorry excuse for a ponytail. Once my feet were shoved into a pair of sneakers, I went downstairs.

Two grim faces greeted me.

I noticed how Abigail and Dippy weren't anywhere to be seen.

The sun was shining brightly through our kitchen window. It illuminated the freshly-scrubbed copper pots and pans, currently drying in the dish drainer. There was no breakfast on the table, though I didn't expect there to be any.

"You have to go to work," I told Dad.

"Taking a personal day."

"Well, where are Dippy and Abby?"

"Visiting Grandma Flannery at the home," Mom answered. "Abigail wasn't ready to go back to school just yet, and Dennis thought it would do him some good to get out."

I cringed.

Grandma Flannery was inherently racist. She was the one who corrupted Dippy into thinking how white people were the only ones who ever did anything. Her stories consistently praised the working-class Irish who built all of New York with their bare hands, and never complained, and then died, the way real men were supposed to. And then, she said, the Negroes came in and destroyed the nuclear family with their single-parent homes, and their children born out of wedlock. She saw Irish families less and less in the neighborhood. They were being taken over, she complained, by gooks, zipper heads, Chinamen, and pan faces, all of whom packed two dozen slant-eyes into one house, and cooked chink food all the time, causing the whole neighborhood to reek of garlic and fish. The towel heads, and rag heads, she explained, those filthy sand niggers, bought up all of the fruit stands and turned them into goddamn Halal markets. Those paved the way for those jihadist terrorists and their fucking mosques. And Grandma Flannery was tired of the beaners, spics, wetbacks, and gringos, standing around on corners looking for illegal work and smoking their reefer. She quickly walked by all of the niggers, coons, jigaboos, and spades, with their ugly tar-babies, determined to not make eye contact with those damn porch monkeys. But the dagos, wops, and grease balls weren't too bad because they were laborers, too, who worshipped at the same Catholic Church, and had identical core values. It was just that they went too crazy over tomatoes instead of potatoes. Besides, her only child, her daughter, married one—my dad—and they had three hybrid Irish-Italian kids. Grandma's worst offenders, though, were the kikes, hebes, and Christ killers who sucked up every penny, and who wore those stupid Jew hats over their big Jew curls. They never showered, Grandma said, because water wasn't free.

When the homos, queers, faggots, and dykes started coming around her neighborhood, Grandma took to becoming a hermit, and she let the Alzheimer's eat away at her brain. Mom and Dad chucked her into a home not long after one of the Christ killers found her having a heated argument with a lamp post, ending in Grandma beating both the rabbi and the lamp post with her purse, stuffed with rocks. My folks put her away so she would stop beating the animate and inanimate alike; so she couldn't keep waking up at three in the morning to drink dishwashing soap and snack on batteries; and, so she would stop stuffing the cat into the microwave. Snowball was sent to the loving home of a sweet, gay cholo couple named Poncho and Enrique. Dippy wanted Grandma to move in with us, causing an even larger rift between the almost-jarhead and myself.

"Grandma Flannery is crazy racist," I whined. My folks shoved me out of the house and into the pickup.

"Stop saying that about your grandmother," Mom warned. "She's old and afflicted with Alzheimer's. She has no idea what she's saying, anymore."

"Then what the hell is her excuse for the other twenty-two years that I've known her?"

"She's set in her ways."

"She made Dippy into a fucking neo-Nazi!"

"He was never a Nazi; cut it out. Don't ever say it again."

"Oh, God." I groaned. "I wanna go back to sleep."

I thumped my forehead against the thick glass of the window. Again, I had been placed in the back.

"Pipe." Dad turned around in the driver's seat to look at me; the whites of his eyes were bloodshot. "There's somewhere we need to, ah, take you."

"I know I'm going to see a shrink, Dad."

"Oh."

He turned back, and glanced at me from the rearview mirror. Dad cocked his head to the side, as if to say *sorry*. I put my head back against the pane of glass separating me from freedom.

It took a half hour to drive to the other side of town, where the hospital was. Dad and I kept quiet, exchanging frequent eye-rolls in the rearview mirror. Mom pretended to sleep. I wanted to ask them if they had settled on some sort of agreement about their marriage. But I thought it was none of my business, despite being an adult and all, because they clearly had certain tensions between them I had never picked up on before.

Denny was always the astute one. He had one hell of a brain, and had fun by proving people wrong with simple logic. Our little sister probably had no promise or potential whatsoever, aside from being a pretty little thing who could dance and walk with books atop her head. Abigail was not interested in music or art. She watched music videos, but kept them on mute, and merely mimicked the choreography.

My family was doomed.

"Piper." Mom woke up from her fake nap and turned down the overhead. She flipped the cover to the mirror, and her reflection met my gaze.

"Yeah?"

"I spoke to the college this morning."

"And what did the college say?" A brow shot up; I wished that they would give me a free ride, given the lightning.

"They're gonna give you Incompletes for the rest of the semester. You'll finish some of your classes in the summer, and the others in the fall."

"What!" My eyes narrowed into slits. I felt tension in my hands and quickly balled them into fists. I wanted to kick the back of her seat; to punch the windows, scream, and call her every four-letter word that I knew.

"It's not the end of the world!" She flipped the cover of the mirror down. "This is what's best for you. For the time being. You have too much in your head, and you need to get over these issues."

"School helps that."

"End of discussion."

"But, Mom—"

"I said, end of discussion."

"Fuck my life."

"You already did."

When we pulled up to the building, I jumped out of the car. My legs firmly stuck to the ground by some invisible, extra-thick bubblegum. Before long, my bottom lip trembled. Overall, I wasn't much of a crier. It was silly and embarrassing, so I kept sad emotional outbursts away from the public.

"Pipe? Hon, are you crying? Need a tissue?" Dad bent his mug close to mine and I recoiled.

"No, I... I have cramps. My period is coming. I'm all right."

He flushed.

Feminine problems always worked as the best excuse. No man ever questioned it.

Mom put a bony hand on my shoulder, and she nudged me forward through the automatic sliding doors. The floors squeaked with each step we took, and the tiles were white with specks of gray. The whole establishment reeked of sanitizer, with the underlying scent of lemon and some sort of flower I couldn't identify. We got on the elevator, and went up six floors, to see the psychiatrist whom my mother picked out for me from the yellow pages.

The narrow hallway on the sixth floor was covered in worn, brown carpet, patterned with green, puce, and yellow diamonds. To annoy my mother, I dragged my feet along the entire stretch until I got up to the receptionist's desk to sign in.

With no other verbalization than a grunt, the receptionist slapped down a clipboard with a lot of dead, thinly-sliced trees on it. I assumed she meant, "If you'd be so kind as to fill out this giant stack of paperwork so we can rape your privacy, it would be much appreciated."

I sucked on my teeth for a moment and scrutinized her appearance. The woman, whose nametag read *Ingrid*, was large and round. Her bright pink face was off-set by her thick ginger hair. She sported a short bob; it did not flatter the beach ball head attached to her millimeter of neck. Ingrid was wearing a rose-colored cardigan, and had an angel pin over her heart with a ruby in the middle.

"July?" I gestured to the brooch.

"Mmph," she eloquently responded.

"I'm July, too. A Leo."

Ingrid blinked at me.

"You're probably a Cancer, right?" My eyes flicked down to the ruby. I wanted to rip the pendant off of her and stab her in her piggy little eyes with it.

My parents, taking no notice, sat on chairs in the waiting room. I could see Mom thumbing through a Cosmopolitan from probably two years back, judging by the cover. Dad was more interested in the daytime talk show on the small television hovering on the ceiling corner.

I twirled back to Ingrid.

"Do you like your job?"

"Mmph."

"I'm guessing 'Mmph' means yes, because you've used it before."

"Piper!" Mom bellowed from behind her magazine. "Damnit, leave the woman alone and fill out your forms!"

"See you soon!" I shouted at Ingrid, who recoiled. She stuffed a chocolate glazed donut into her immense trap.

The paperwork was insane. There were thirty sheets to fill out, back and forth. Every question imaginable was on them. Once the easy, Patriot Act stuff was out of the way, like name, address, social security number, and health care provider, I got to the real bologna of the form.

"Have you ever been in a cult?" I read aloud.

"It does not ask if you've ever been in a cult, for Christ's sake," Mom bitched.

I pointed out the question, number thirty-seven, and Mom frowned.

"You should write down 'Blue Oyster Cult.'" Dad smiled; he was proud of his quick wit, and I was, too.

"Christ Almighty, Bruno," Mom snapped. "This isn't a joke."

I wrote it down, anyway.

On the form, I checked off "yes" to schizophrenia, nymphomania, kleptomania, bulimia, anorexia, and trichotillomania: the compulsion of pulling out one's hair.

Of course, I had none of those. My hair was proof enough.

Under the "other" category, I filled in: fear of closed spaces, sweatshirts, baseballs, snow cones, lint, and fear of persons named Ingrid.

With the last swoop of the O in my last name, I un-stuck myself from the plastic chair and sauntered over to Ingrid, who was munching on celery.

"I don't think," I cheerfully smiled. "That celery will necessarily negate the calories in the donut you wolfed down." I dropped the clipboard down on her desk. I didn't care. What did I have to lose, anyway?

Returning to the plastic chair, I dropped my head onto my dad's shoulder, and closed my eyes for a few moments. I was royally pissed off that my college handed me Incom-pletes for the rest of the semester, because my mother in-formed them about my attempted suicide. It bugged me how she relayed personal information behind my back, but what irked me even more was how I actually wanted to be in class. School was a wonderful distraction from the tiresome, awful situation at home.

My eyes snapped open again when I heard barking. I loved dogs, so I looked around in search for one, figuring there was maybe a blind patient with a service shepherd.

Instead, sitting directly across from me, was a man wearing a red collar. He was a clone of Santa Claus, only without the beard, and with crossed eyes. When he glimpsed me, or what I assumed was looking at me, because I couldn't tell, he let out another bark. I glanced around for his owner, but he appeared to be on his own.

"Jesus Christ," I said to Dad. He quickly wrapped his arm around my shoulders.

Even Mom was inching closer to him.

Within minutes, a slew of mental degenerates filed into the place.

I saw head-pickers, nose-diggers, nail-biters. There were shakers, criers, screamers, and the solitary barker. For the most part, they kept to themselves, though the noises and tics were disturbing.

"Piper." A voice sounded from the corridor. "Piper Marino."

I rolled my eyes at my mother, and patted Dad on the hand as I left them in the midst of the heavy traffic of the mentally disturbed.

The voice called my name again, and I followed, finding it to be a sickening game of hide and seek.

"Hello," I muttered. I entered the cramped office and blinked at the gentleman in his late fifties; he had salt-and-pepper hair, green eyes, and stubby fingernails. He was wearing a pale blue, button-down shirt, and a tie decorated with little pictures of donuts. I wondered what the donut-obsession meant, but refrained from asking. I wasn't there to take an interest in the psychiatry bullshit.

"Ms. Marino, I presume?" he chuckled. "Have a seat."

"You presume correctly, Holmes." I slinked into the

poorly-cushioned seat across from the shrink, and slouched down.

"I'm Dr. Robert Bromley, and I'm glad to meet you."

I glanced at him, though my eyes were quickly distracted by the clutter in his office. He had a box of pink tissues on his desk, along with a Rubik's Cube, mountains of rubber bands, thick stacks of paperwork, and a framed photograph of himself holding up a giant fish. The rest of the room was occupied by various cardboard boxes, trinkets and knickknacks, dust, and a lone poster of a kitten, in a basket, with spaghetti piled atop its head.

"There's a lot of stuff in here," I observed.

"Is that going to be a problem, ah, Ms. Marino?"

"Piper."

"Piper," he nodded. "I see here that you have claustrophobia. And, ah, a slew of other phobias as well."

"I think I'll be okay, you know, for now."

The doctor leaned back in his chair; arms folded behind his head, he displayed his drooping pit stains.

"Why don't you tell me what's brought you here today, Piper?"

"Well." I sighed. "My parents forced me. I'm a failed suicide. Maybe they're covering their asses in case I get the urge to do it again." I scratched the nape of my neck, and then propped the red hood from my sweatshirt atop my head.

Dr. Bromley grabbed a black ballpoint, and hurriedly

transcribed what I was saying onto a legal pad. Or at least that's what I thought he was doing. His chicken-scratch writing was illegible.

"Do you currently feel suicidal?"

"At this very moment, no. I'm more concerned with making it out of here without the barking guy outside taking a piss on my leg or something. You know, marking territory and stuff."

The shrink didn't even chuckle. His appearance was dead serious, and the concern was bulging from his eyes.

"Let's, ah, just take a quick once-over of your paperwork." The doctor thumbed through the forms. His lips got thinner and thinner as he continued to read on. "You were in a cult called Blue Oyster, correct?"

"Um." I shrugged. "Yeah, sure. Why not."

"And what did you do in this cult?"

"We mostly just, um, didn't fear the reaper."

"I'm sorry?"

"Skip number thirty-seven." I dismissively waved my hand. "It's a joke. You know, the band."

"I'm not familiar." Bromley jotted down more notes.

I had never been a fan of psychiatrists, psychologists, or therapists. When the news came back to us how Dippy had his leg blown off and almost died, we'd all gone to a counseling center for families of injured or dead soldiers. I had always been chastised by my mom for not opening up, or for giving sarcastic, snarky answers.

Bromley didn't seem too keen on me, either.

"Ms. Marino—ah, Piper—it seems as though you're a habitual liar, which stems from compulsive lying. Now, this most likely began in your early childhood…"

"Whoa, okay. Hang on." I sat up in the seat and flashed the international sign for *time out*. "Let me stop you there. I was, you know, joking on the forms."

"That's lying. Compulsively."

"It's goofing off."

"But why?"

"Because I don't want to be here!" I shouted. Bromley appeared almost smug, getting under my skin immediately.

"Did you really attempt suicide?" Dr. Bromley asked.

"Yes," I replied.

"Is this part here true—your brother is a wounded veteran?"

"Yes."

"Your parents are having marital difficulties?"

"Yes."

"You're a middle child… and you were struck by lightning?"

"Yes."

"Is there anything else you need to tell me so we can work this out?"

"Yes."

"What is it?"

"The Devil's son is after me."

"Excuse me for a moment." Bromley hauled ass out of his office, so I took the opportunity to snoop around the room, making sure his plaques and certificates were the real deal. Much to my dismay, they appeared legitimate. Most of them were caked in dust, so I dragged my finger along one of the bigger ones and wrote "I Love Ingrid," except I drew a heart instead of writing out the word "Love."

When I slipped back into my seat, I noticed how the doctor had two people walking behind him. My folks.

"Uh-uh." I shook my head. "No deal, they aren't allowed in here. I'm over eighteen." I glared at my mother; I was unwilling to give her an inch, since she had taken away so much in just one phone call.

"I think it would be best if your parents heard what you had to say," Bromley insisted.

"No, okay? I signed the privacy act thing and I'm not allowing this."

"Pipe?" Dad poked his head in the doorway. "Are you sure about this?"

I nodded. "I'm sure, Dad."

"Jesus," Mom muttered. "She just complicates everything."

"Have it your way," the shrink said to me. Bromley saw both of my stressed parents out of the room, and he shut the door behind him. He shuffled over to his ancient wooden desk and plopped down on his chair. It was probably still warm from his body fermenting in the seat for hours.

I brought one of my legs up and put my foot on my other knee, and suspiciously scrutinized him.

"You don't think it would be useful to have your parents here, to help sort out your issues?"

"No."

"Why not?"

"Because they have enough going on in their lives. This isn't easy for them, and it sure as shit isn't easy for me." I shifted in my seat. "Besides, we—you and I—just met. Already you want to bring two more people into this stellar session?"

"Perhaps you're right." Bromley folded his hands atop his desk. He leaned forward. "You seem to be quite the independent young woman." His coffee breath shot me back a few inches.

"With a mother like that, with a father always gone, and siblings I can't rely on, and no friends; well, yeah, I'd better be independent, or nothing would ever move forward."

"Except suicide?"

"Right."

We stared at each other for a few moments; my eyes were narrowed in anger, and his were pools of questions. The whole Devil thing must have intrigued him, I figured. It seemed like something he probably didn't hear, though judging by his clientele, I couldn't have been so sure.

"We'll just switch topics here for a moment. You, ah, say the Devil's son is after you?" His eyes flickered, and I could sense that he wanted to smile.

"Yeah. He is."

"Why is he after you, Piper?"

"Because." I exhaled loudly. "My suicide didn't pan out as expected. He collects the souls of the suicides or something—I don't know the details—it's just hard to talk to him. He's, like, intimidating, and I think I might have a crush on him. I mean, how sick and perverse is that, you know? But if you saw him, you'd probably understand. Not that I'm, like, implying that you're a homosexual or anything. Even if you were, though, it would be kind of cool. In fact, I might, actually, kind of not hate you so much if you were."

Dr. Bromley blinked quickly, and many times.

"I'm married to a woman," he croaked.

"So is Jerry."

"Jerry is the son of the Devil?"

"No," I groaned. "Jerry is my suicide hotline friend."

"So who's the Devil's son?"

"His name is Lucian." I thought about what Lucian had told me—how his real name was in a language I didn't understand. He was intriguing, to say the very least. Of course, there were about a million questions I wanted to ask him, but he didn't seem to be the Q-and-A type of guy.

"Lucian?" Bromley scribbled on his pad. "As in Luciano? Light? It means Light. How can the son of the Devil have a name meaning Light?"

"I don't know." I shrugged. "Lucifer means Lightbringer, so, it's not, you know, a huge stretch."

"Do you actually see Lucian, or does he talk to you inside of your head?"

I scratched my head, and thought how insane the doctor was. Okay, sure, I was the one who was seeing a demon, but the psychiatrist seemed like a total mental patient, too.

"No, he talks to me in dreams. Well, he talked to me once in a dream, and then once in person, out on my balcony," I explained. "Oh, but then he went into my bedroom."

The shrink flicked his gaze over to a battered, old doll that was perched on his bookshelf. "I'm going to ask you a question." He straightened his back out. "Was there inappropriate sexual contact?"

"Jesus! No!" My cheeks reddened.

"I see. So, this—Lucian—he came to you on your balcony when you tried to commit suicide?"

"No," I said. "Last night."

"What did he say to you?"

"He got all mad at me for accidentally making Holy Water by saying a prayer when I was drinking. It burned him, you know, so he got all pissy about it. But it'll be

okay. He's gonna show me what happened when I died."
I flicked a ball of lint off of my shoulder and watched it
land atop the box of tissues.

"Uh-huh."

"I haven't gone on a trip since the family vacation to
Washington. D.C., not the state." I fumbled with the
strings on my sweatshirt. "I'm assuming that it's gonna be
really warm in Hell. That would be the correct assump-
tion, wouldn't it? Hell is hot, and Heaven is just right? It
makes sense to me."

Bromley, appearing completely flabbergasted, helplessly raised his hands.

"I mean," I continued. "It's not like I'll wear a bikini
down there. But I'm thinking a tank top and, maybe, a
pair of shorts. My running sneakers, obviously."

"I'd like to start you on some medication, immediately," Dr. Bromley stated. He grabbed a prescription pad
and scribbled. "Clozapine will help."

"What's Clozapine?"

"An antipsychotic."

"No."

"Hm?" The shrink stopped writing, and gaped at me.
His bushy brows were raised, and he was even crankier
than he was when I asked about the gay issue.

"I'm not psychotic," I insisted. "Therefore, I don't
need to take any antipsychotics."

"Perhaps a benzodiazepine."

"No."

"Are you refusing?"

"Yes, I am."

"All right." He picked up a sterling-silver pen. "I'm going to have to refer you to a psychologist, then."

"Nah," I shrugged. "This wasn't helpful. The next round won't be, either. I'll just, you know, end up getting stuck with another one of you overpaid assholes." I was already going to Hell—what did it matter? "And, by the way, you have too much shit in here; what are you, a fucking hoarder or something? You need a stronger antiperspirant, your tie is stupid, and the place needs to be cleaned. You have the bitchiest fucking receptionist ever, who needs to, like, get the gigantic stick pulled out of her gigantic ass—"

"She's my wife!"

My jaw went slack. I didn't know whether to laugh, or to extend my deepest condolences. Shaking my head, I got up from the chair and smoothed out my shirt.

"You poor bastard." It was a phrase I always wanted to use. "Or maybe it's Ingrid who's the poor one."

Leaving the doctor behind, I went back into the waiting area, and inclined my head toward my parents. The dog-man was eyeing a fake plant in the corner, and I figured it would be best to leave before he decided he needed to relieve himself.

On the way out, I waved to Ingrid.

"Bitch," she mumbled.

"Enjoy your marriage," I retorted. My middle fingers ascended.

"Mr. and Mrs. Marino!" Bromley called; he had left his office and sauntered into the hallway. "I need a word."

Ten minutes later, I was shoved through the door by my parents.

12

Transition

MOM, DAD, AND I stopped for breakfast on the way home. Our favorite diner was relatively empty, save for tired-looking waitresses. My parents sat beside each other, pleasantly surprising me, and I slid into the booth across from them. Maybe the dog-man had scared them close, again. In general, I knew Mom was disappointed and angry, and Dad really needed sleep because he was a zombie. He had always been a fairly quiet man, and I knew he was trying to keep it all together for the rest of us. I couldn't imagine what he was feeling. His wife didn't want him around anymore, his oldest daughter tried to kill herself, his youngest daughter was already turning into her mother, and his only son had his leg blown off in a war that made no sense, leaving him a shell of his former self. On top of it all, he worked all the time and forked over his paycheck each week to provide for us, the parasites. He was the host, and we were leeching.

I ordered chocolate chip pancakes with a large glass of chocolate milk. My parents had eggs, scrambled, with bacon and toast. They opted for coffee.

"Do you want to tell us what you talked about with the doctor? Or why you refuse to go back?" Mom inquired.

"No."

"Well, do you wanna know why they won't ever take you back?"

"I already know."

"And why is that?"

"Because." I took the paper placemat and made an origami fortune-teller. "I insulted the doctor, his wife, his office, his practice, psychiatry as a whole; and, because everything I said was true, which, clearly, he can't handle. I think Freud might've mentioned a link between self-consciousness and size." I looked up at my parents. "Do you have a pen?"

Dad stared down into his cup of Joe.

"Dad."

He leaned closer to the black liquid.

"Dad."

His nose was an inch away from the coffee.

"Dad!"

"Huh?"

"*Christ*," Mom muttered under her breath.

"Do you have a pen, Dad?"

"No, kiddo." He probably wanted to dive, head-first, into the burning hot coffee.

"Mom? Pen?"

Mom ignored my request for a writing utensil. "I don't know why you have to piss people off all the time."

"It's my nature."

I wanted to tell her to consider it an inherited trait. A Flannery one. But, instead, I glanced over at Dad, who didn't seem to be registering the conversation. He appeared to be far away, vacant, and was still red-eyed. I surmised that he was on auto-pilot, and had been ever since he collected me from the lightning strike. I hated the guilt I carried with me about the event, and I knew how nothing I could do would ever fix the situation. Certainly not psychiatric sessions with Bromley.

"What's wrong with you?" Mom wondered.

"I thought," I continued. "Maybe offing myself would remedy it all."

"We all love you," Mom insisted. She brought her coffee mug up to her lips, blowing on the surface of the liquid. "And we want you here. Alive, healthy, and happy. I carried you around for nine months, suffered through seven hours of labor, and stopped sleeping and eating to take care of you. I brought you into this world with the hope that you would make the best life for yourself. Not for you to piss it all away."

"Sorry." I wanted to tell Mom how she was just shy of eloquent.

"Are you really sorry? Or are you just saying you're sorry?"

"What's the difference, Mom?"

"Either you mean it, or you don't."

"Does it matter to you which one it is, as long as you get an apology?"

"It does."

"Dad?"

"Huh?"

"Does it matter?"

He had no idea what I was talking about. Dad gave a non-commital shoulder-raise, and busied himself with toast.

I stuffed a big bite of pancake into my mouth so I could mull it over. I was truly sorry for turning the snow-globe of their lives upside-down. I wasn't sorry for doing what I felt was necessary. I was sorry for the repercussions. But I wasn't sorry that everyone got a wake-up call.

I swallowed the mushed pancake. "I'm half-sorry."

Mom put down her mug. "What's half-sorry?"

"It's—I mean—I feel bad that I put you guys through

shit."

"But?"

"But, in my head, there's justification."

"And you don't wanna talk about that?" Mom wondered.

"No. Not now."

"Bruno!" Mom snapped.

Dad jumped; he knocked his knee against the table. "What?"

Mom shot the death-stare at him. "What are we supposed to do now?"

"Wait for this place to get held up," I suggested. "So I can die honorably while defending the diner, and taking a bullet to the head."

"PIPER!" Mom bellowed.

Our waitress, a brunette about my age, hurried over to the table.

"Are you folks all right?"

"Check, please," Dad piped in.

The waitress shuffled away.

"Let's just finish our food," I suggested. "Pay the bill, and then go home."

WHEN WE ARRIVED BACK at the house, I noticed the car was back. Contrary to what a lot of people believed, my brother was more than capable of driving. I still thought I was a much better driver than he was, because I had perfected parallel parking, but he wasn't the worst.

We walked into the house, and Mom hurriedly went into the kitchen to chain-smoke and bake cookies, and Dad retired to the garage to hammer at things. I saw Abby perched on the sofa. She was wearing a poofy marshmallow skirt, with pink and yellow flowers bedazzled with gaudy, fake jewels.

I grabbed a bottle of water and flopping down beside her. "What the fuck are you wearing?"

"Clothes," she responded. Abigail frowned at me and muted the television.

"Where's Dippy?"

"How come you always ask that?"

"It's a habit."

"He's sleeping downstairs."

I wanted to go wake him up and tell him all about the dog-man, Ingrid, and Bromley. He would probably get a kick out of the trifecta, but he was probably worn out from babysitting Abby all day, and being around the old folks in the home. Neither of us was fond of visiting the place where senior citizens go to die. The smell of pee and sanitizer hit us as soon as we stepped inside. The old folks descended upon us like it was the zombie apocalypse, thinking we were related to them. They hacked up phlegm, smelled like death masked with baby powder, and they gummed bright shades of Jell-O. A few tried to reach out and touch us, but we always recoiled in horror. It was awful enough how I had to kiss my grandmother's sunken-in, cold cheek.

"Did Grandma say anything stupid to you?" I wondered.

"I don't know."

"Did she talk about Hitler?"

"I don't know. Wait. Yeah."

I rolled my eyes and clicked my tongue. Even though she was living with Alzheimer's, my grandmother was still a racist pain in the ass. I didn't like how she had spewed her venomous hatred of all non-Irish folk to Denny, back when he was impressionable and confused. The same thing could have happened to Abigail, so I didn't want her going to the nursing home without me there to supervise. Ideally, I didn't want her going at all. Dippy was too much of a pacifist and wouldn't fire back at Grandma. It was why he wasn't written out of her will like I was.

"What did she say about Hitler?"

"Um." Abigail glanced over at me, and slowly moved her judgmental eyes over my attire. "She said, um, he saw his girlfriend's auto-topsy and became a vegetarian."

"Autopsy," I corrected. "How the hell does Grandma remember that, but she can't remember how old she is, or what she ate for breakfast, or what Dad's name is?"

Abby shrugged. "What's an autopsy?"

"I'll tell you when you're older."

She crossed her arms over her chest and slouched back

against the sofa.

"Okay," I shrugged. "It's when you cut open the body of a dead—"

"No!" She covered her ears with her hands, and shook her head from side to side. She had wanted to know the answer, and I provided that for her.

I removed her hands from her ears. "Trust me, kiddo; if I say how I'll tell you something when you're older, I'll tell you when I know you're ready. Cool?"

Abby nodded. "Cool." She watched me intently, maybe unsure of what to ask next. "Piper," she quietly said. "Why'd you try to kill yourself for?"

Sure, Abby had cried when I was in the hospital and all, but I didn't think she actually, truly, gave one iota of a shit. After all, it would have been a whole lot easier if I wasn't around, anymore. It would mean more things for her. Attention, stupid frilly clothes, and the car once she was old enough.

Taking a moment to think it over, so I could explain it properly to an eight-year-old, I tapped my fingers against my knee to collect my thoughts.

"Well, there were a few reasons."

"Like what?"

"Like, um. You know, I didn't want to get older and watch your lives get all screwed up."

Abigail pursed her lip and furrowed her brow. She seemed to be thinking hard about what I had said. She completely ignored the television, the smell of cookie dough wafting into the room, and the alluring promise of fun she could be having by learning how to polish silver instead of hanging around her depressed older sister.

"But," Abby frowned. "Who says that our lives will get screwed up?"

"Well, um, I just figured they would."

"Why?"

"I. I don't know. I guess because, you know, there just doesn't seem to be any other way around it. I know, like, you're eight and all but you're not a dumb kid. Can't you see how messed up this family is?" I looked intently at my little sister. She was a miniature version of me. And maybe she wasn't meaner. Maybe I was the mean one for not giving her time and attention, anymore. For not caring, or doing anything, about my mother essentially making her into this pageant queen. Without a doubt, though, Abigail was much more beautiful than I was.

After mulling it over, Abby spoke. "Well, yeah. But I know about a lot more messed up families than ours. Like Sarah's. She has two moms."

"It isn't messed up."

"It's weird."

"It's not what you're used to, is all. There are all different kinds of families. But love is love, right? No matter what it seems like to other people."

Abby mulled it over. "I guess."

"Well, it's true."

"And, like," she continued. "There are those poor people in the world who don't even have houses, and they have flies all over them. You know? The tar-babies."

"The—the what?"

"The tar-babies," she repeated. I had heard her correctly.

"Okay," I frowned. "Don't ever use that phrase again."

"Why?"

"Because it's racist. And mean, and hurtful, and I know Grandma taught it to you, so, no, I'm not going to get you in any trouble. Just promise you won't say it again."

"Okay. I promise."

We exchanged glances, and, in that moment, my eyes stung. I wanted to protect her from all of the vile things in the world, but I knew it was impossible. Abigail was going to grow up, and would have the choice to follow in the crazy footsteps of our relatives, or break away and make something better of herself. Though I wished against all odds it was the latter, there was still a major chance she could turn out to be completely fucked in the head.

"At least we live here and have each other," Abby broke the silence. "And that's love. Right?"

"It is." I nodded. "It definitely is." It was the smartest thing I had ever heard and it came from an eight-year-old whose favorite activity was swinging her hips around like the girls in music videos. "So you think everything will be okay, then? With the family, I mean."

"Yeah." Abby twirled a lock of hair around her finger. "Just as long as we stick together."

"Hmm."

"Pipe?"

"Yeah?"

"Why are you asking me so many questions?"

I put my hand on top of her head to ruffle her hair. She wasn't fond of her hair being messed up, but she also didn't mind so much, because it meant she was given attention.

"Thanks, Abby."

"For what?"

"Everything."

"You're welcome." She glanced at me suspiciously, though something had shifted. Abigail, being just a kid, was constantly changing. She went from being more like a daughter, back when our mom had gone off the deep end, to my worst nightmare, when Mom had reclaimed her status as head bitch in charge. It had been a difficult transition for me. Even though I hated being a single housewife and mother, part of me knew how I had it in me to be a caregiver. When it'd been yanked out from beneath me, my bitterness overflowed. Abigail had to have picked up on it, drawing her even closer to my mother. Though I still took on the burden of some responsibilities,

I was no longer needed to tuck her in, or read her a story, or teach her long division.

"Pipe?"

"Yeah, kiddo?"

"Why do you hate Grandma?"

"I don't hate Grandma. I don't particularly like Grandma. But I think, maybe, hate is too strong a word to use. She's just—she hates a lot of people for stupid reasons, and it upsets me."

"Do you hate any of us?"

"No." I shook my head. "Of course not. I love all of you."

"Really?"

"Yeah. With all my heart."

"Then you shouldn't have tried to kill yourself."

"I know. I'm sorry." I wrapped my arms around her. Neither of us cared about how I was squashing her dress. I took the remote from the sofa and cranked the volume back up to normal. I changed the channel to cartoons, because she needed to be a kid, and so did I.

13

Lucian

LUCIAN RETURNED AT NIGHT. I was in my bedroom, thumbing through my CD collection, when he came up behind me and breathed fire down my neck.

"I wish you wouldn't do that," I groaned.

"Liar," he murmured into my ear.

"Shut up."

"No one talks back to me."

"Yeah, well, I just did. Like I have anything to lose by talking back." I whirled around and stared at him, my head tilting up to meet his eyes. They appeared darker than I had remembered. The rest of him was still the same, though; and, again, he wore the same button-down black shirt. "I bet you hate clothes," I commented.

"Yes," Lucian replied.

"I can tell. You seem the type."

"It's our nature."

I bit down on my lip, and pressed play on the stereo. After a second, *Moonlight Sonata* filled my room. I didn't know why I was so calm around him; after all, he was basically Hell's repo man.

"Hm." Lucian touched his chin with his thumb and index finger. "You're a fan of this type of music? *Moonlight Sonata*. I haven't heard it in many years. I had been taking the soul of this woman…"

My eyes widened. Lucian was actually opening up to me, and it was pretty exciting. The son of the Devil must have millions of stories—all of them fascinating in their own right.

"Please," I urged. "Continue."

Lucian glared at me, though he wanted to tell me his story. After all, it didn't seem as though he had to deal with my type of situation often. In a way, I liked it. I felt special—special to this being, this inhuman man, who was granting me a special insight into what he did for a living. I was sure it was a rarity; after all, Lucian didn't strike me as the type of guy who opened up very often.

"Okay. I'll tell you."

He moved onto my bed after I did, though he sprawled on his back as though he owned it. Perhaps he did—if it belonged to me and I belonged to him, surely my possessions were as good as his. The bed was queen-sized, and I had bright purple sheets over it, along with purple accents here and there; a purple lamp, alarm clock, area rug, and garbage pail. The Azzurri poster contrasted wonderfully.

Lucian unbuttoned his shirt, slowly and deliberately. He wanted me to spy him. After all, he had the most striking body I had ever seen. Even Lucian himself said he knew what he looked like, therefore could understand why women were so drawn to him. I tried to not feel jealous, but the jealousy was quickly pushed away in favor of red-blooded ogling. Lucian got to his last button and unfastened it. I watched in awe as the black material merely just glided off of him, as if being taken away by some delicate, invisible source.

I tried to be as comfortable as possible. It didn't work because this beefy, muscular guy was occupying most of the area. I ended up huddled up by his waist, my knees drawn up to my chest. I took up little space, though I condensed myself even more by wrapping my arms around myself and resting my knees on my chin. I could see Lucian's smirk.

"Once upon a time…"

"Once upon a time," Lucian took over; his sultry voice was perfect for monologues. "In a time period not too far away, and in a place not too far away, there was a suicide.

It was nineteen twenty-nine, and the location was Mahattan. The Upper East Side, to be exact. That era was as miserable as this one, although technology was, of course, a mere fraction of what it is today. I preferred the look, then. People used their thumbs less often."

I grinned.

"Today, there are many distractions from what is going on around you. Then, the biggest distraction was Coney Island. And, when that wasn't enough, they jumped from windows."

I nodded at Lucian, not wanting him to think I was some sort of idiot. I knew all about the Great Depression—the fall of Wall Street. We were currently living through its second incarnation, so I was familiar with the goings-on of the late nineteen-twenties.

"But I digress," he continued. "I was alerted that there was going to be a soul in need of collection. The apartment the family lived in was posh. I had gone straight into the bathroom, where my soul-to-collect was almost ripe for the picking. The bathtub was filled with ice-cold water, and the lights had been dimmed considerably. As I bent forward to snatch out the soul, I heard—"

"—*Moonlight Sonata.*"

"Oh, were you there, Piper? Would you like to finish the story?"

"No, no. I'm sorry. Go on, please."

Lucian sighed. He probably thought he was on

babysitting duty, rather than soul-collecting duty.

"*Moonlight Sonata*." He finally got to say it. "It was from across the apartment. Soft, melodic, and very much on target. I was impressed. Still, I didn't let the music distract me from my job. I took the soul out of her body and placed it beside me, leaving everything else intact. The bath, the hairdryer…"

"She electrocuted herself?" I paled.

"Yes."

"And I electrocuted myself. And I'm a female."

"Yes," Lucian confirmed.

"Are you, like, assigned to girls who zap themselves to death?"

Lucian gritted his teeth. I supposed I had struck a nerve, but I did find their entire system to be wondrous. The urge to ask him more questions was nagging my guts.

"Well?"

"Something like that," Lucian responded.

"Let's say I blew my head off with a gun instead. Would you be the one to come and get me?"

"You're asking too many questions." His nose flared. "I'm frustrated with all of this, and I still haven't finished my story yet—the story you begged me to tell. Do you remember?"

I went red in the cheeks, and pathetically nodded, so he could continue.

"Right," Lucian said. "She was shaking when she saw

her dead body, as most of them do. I wonder about the mortal mind sometimes—what do they anticipate? The afterlife follows your core set of beliefs, and how they were executed. Why do you think that free will was put into place? For example, you're a Catholic." Lucian's lips thinned. "A Catholic who kills his or herself cannot be forgiven. Ticket to Hell. An atheist, on the other hand, who believes in nothing, gets nothing when they die. It was the choice they secured, and they will have to suffer the consequences of it when they die. Those who follow all the rules go to Heaven—not very densely populated, or so I hear—Buddhists get Nirvana. Most mortals end up in Purgatory. You make your choice here, and you reap it when your body is gone, and only your soul is left."

I was awed. So if I hadn't tried to kill myself, maybe I could have gone off to Heaven, to meet my grandparents. To see my dead dog, Shoes, who died when I was a kid. How miserable.

"So," Lucian went on. "I dragged her down into Hell. She was screaming for her brother, who was in the next room playing the piano. I explained to her how he couldn't hear her, though he would be the one to discover her body. And then he would end up killing himself, too, because he was secretly in love with her. People think Hell is sick? The insanity begins right here, and then it's carried over. But I digress. That was why she ended her life: guilt, because, the night before, she had decided to succumb and sleep with her brother." Lucian actually chuckled when he concluded.

"I thought she did it because of the money situation—you said it was nineteen twenty-nine."

"Yes, but this particular incident had nothing to do with the Great Depression. Well, it had to be a depression for the both of them." Lucian grabbed a bottle of cold water from my bedside, and took a drink.

"What happened when the brother killed himself?"

"He was taken down, as well. A reverse-magnetic field was placed around them. They couldn't touch, kiss, or even be near each other. For eternity. It's been—what? Almost ninety years now, and they still cry, and wail, constantly. Irksome."

I shuddered. I didn't want to go to Hell. I didn't want to get beaten or whipped—I had a low tolerance for pain, and always cried like a little girl whenever I stubbed my toe.

What I needed was a subject change. I stared at Lucian's half-naked body. "Why do you bother wearing them at all?" I gestured to his shirt.

"People tend to panic when they see naked men walking around. Not that I care about them, but…"

"You mean other people can see you?"

"Of course."

There I was, thinking Lucian was invisible to everyone except me. He just came across as the proverbial devil on your shoulder, the one who whispered naughty things into your ear, and left you with the desire to set something on fire. The look Lucian sported told me how I was an even bigger idiot than I ever imagined.

"But I can be invisible if I want to," he added.

"But, because you look like that, why would you choose invisibility?"

I saw a flicker of a smile tug at Lucian's lips, but he neither confirmed nor denied.

"So..." I got up from the bed, and sat down on my computer chair, wheeling over to him. "Have there been any more, um, advances in this whole taking-my-soul stuff? Because, listen, maybe you can just... you know, let me keep my soul and live. And I'll call off the whole tour of Hell and death thing. When I die for real, it pretty much will be a guarantee I'm going south, anyway." I wished for some sort of redemption.

"I don't want to stand around waiting, Piper. I'm not patient. Yes, you're a suicide. And, because of your choices, you get a one-way ticket straight down. No stops. No questions. Nothing." He flicked his eyes over to me.

I took a deep breath, slowly letting out the trapped air. My options were limited, unless a miracle decided to happen. "When?"

"Right now," Lucian muttered. He left his shirt on my bed, and I couldn't help but stare at his muscles. The tattoos he had on each arm were pure works of art. I wondered if he'd had them done by a mortal or by some tattoo shack down around Styx.

"So, wait a second. You're going to take me to Hell, right?"

"Right."

"And show me what I saw when I died."

"Yes."

"And then what?"

Lucian looked over at me and grabbed my wrist. He yanked me close to him, seated me on his lap, and moved his hand to my chest, touching my scar. My heart was pounding hard and fast; it wanted to push right through my chest and expose itself to Lucian. It would have cried, "Take me, love me, cherish me, I'm yours." But that didn't happen. Instead, I shifted awkwardly on the demon's lap, and gaped at him the way he stared at me—slowly, deliberately, intrusive.

"And then, I take your soul."

"How?"

"The same way you did it the first time around, except I'll be present. As soon as your soul leaves your body, I grab hold of it, and you and I take the ride down." Lucian was knowledgeable about it all, and I wondered how many times he had gone through this. It was frightening to think about.

"Why the replay?"

"Rules."

"Hell has rules?"

"Yes."

"So I'm actually going to be dead—just when I want to live—and I have to get electrocuted again. You're going to take my soul away and, uh, do what with it, exactly?" It was a fair question.

"You'll receive tags." He moved his fingers down the length of Dippy's dog tags, and held them in the palm of his hand for a moment, reading the inscription. "Not unlike these. They'll have your name, method of death, and the collector - my name, Lucian, will be next to it."

I bit down on my lip. "Will it say Lucian or your real name?"

"Lucian. It's what I go by. My birth name is Mesopotamian, and it's not easy to pronounce. Need to fit in with the ever-evolving culture." He glanced at me, and I actually smiled. I didn't know why, but Lucian had me grinning. Maybe it was the elfin ears.

"Do I, you know, live with you or something? What am I going to be doing for eternity down there in Hell?"

"My father oversees it all. Think of him as, ah, the president. My brothers and I are his soldiers. Enforcers, if you will." Lucian appeared to be proud of himself. He was sitting up, still, and flexing his muscles as he spoke. "Hell isn't a lot different from Earth. It's smaller. You will see things that are going to scare you—the way you see things here that scare you. True Hell isn't *exactly* Dante's vision of it. But, despite the day-to-day, you will be punished for the sins and transgressions you committed here. As a suicide, you will feel pain. You will be whipped for giving up the precious gift of life."

"Is there a river of Styx? And Charon? And Cerberus?" I inquired. I was nauseous thinking about being whipped for eternity.

"Not exactly," he admitted. "But there are horrors. Things you could never imagine. Far beyond what you have already seen."

I widened my eyes. "It was real?"

"Of course it was real."

A knot formed in my stomach. My body was paralyzed. I couldn't catch my breath.

With a groan, Lucian pressed his hand against my heart and pushed. I breathed normally again; slowly and evenly.

"Thanks." I paused for a beat. "Won't my family notice I've gone off with you?"

"No. Our time is different. We're going to be down there for a time, but it'll be less than a second to them. They'll have no idea."

I was amazed by that piece of information. A week of being trapped in Hell is just enough time to microwave a mini-bag of popcorn. Maybe.

I got up and put on my sneakers, knowing that there was no other option. Because I was expecting it to be warm down in Hell, I pulled off my sweatshirt, leaving me in my white tank top and jeans. I re-fastened my ponytail.

"You look like you're going to a volleyball game," he grumbled.

"Yeah, well." I rolled my eyes. "You look like you're going to some porn convention."

"Touché."

"How do we get out—"

No sooner had I asked my question, or tried to, Lucian grabbed hold of me, tightly, and forced me to close my eyes. We were whirling down, down, down. It was getting warm, but not to the point of sweating. Maybe it was just my body pressed up against his hot, bare skin. I wondered if Lucian had fire coursing through his veins instead of blood. Anything was possible.

When we stopped, my feet hit ground. It was soft. I once again smelled incense and the thick dew. In the far distance, I heard a wail. I knew precisely where I was.

"Gates of Hell," Lucian stated.

14

Animam Edere

WE WERE BACK WHERE I first remembered meeting Lucian. The trees were back, only they appeared a lot more terrifying than I had ever imagined. Tall, wide, and dense, they loomed over me. Even the sky was blacker and I could have sworn the stars were dimmer than they had been. But it could have just been my imagination.

Lucian nudged me forward, and our feet padded against the thick, green grass. He was barefoot, and wearing the same torn, black pants I recalled from our first meeting. I didn't bother questioning it. As we walked forward, a mild wind whooshed through the treetops, ruffling the leaves and making a soft whistling sound. My companion paid no mind to any of it.

"Hey, Lucian, this is the spot where we met. Right here." I stopped on the spot and inhaled the smell of incense. Water vapor danced in the air. I could see the glossy dew on the tips of the blades of grass. It was serene, though I could not stop the sense of foreboding coursing through my veins.

"Yes." Lucian's eyes darted around.

"What are you searching for?"

"Nothing."

He grabbed hold of my shoulder and pushed me forward, through the black gates. His eyes were constantly shifting, as if he was preparing to get ambushed by something. If he was feeling anxious, then my own anxiety was amplified. After all, he was the one who knew the place, and I was simply nothing more than a tourist.

The wailing became louder and louder as we walked. Soon enough, I could make out both a male and a female voice. I knew it had to be the brother and sister who had killed themselves.

"Suicides," Lucian growled.

We entered a clearing and met hundreds of pairs of eyes. I had been wondering where all of the souls were; though, if I could have taken it back, I would have. They were all sullen, with the most terrifying facial contortions of despair I had ever seen. Some of them had their mouths hanging open in a permanent grimace. I could see the dark red splotches of blood on their bodies, dripping from deep, elongated slashes. My body trembled, and even the presence of Lucian's hand on my back did nothing to remedy my panic.

"They aren't translucent or anything," I whispered.

"No," Lucian stated. "The soul isn't translucent or transparent. Invisible to the human eye, yes. But solid."

We pushed our way through the crowd, and I clung to Lucian. The grimaces contorted into horrifying scowls; they were hissing and sneering at Lucian as we passed. To the right of us were a line of six people getting whipped by two intense men. One had blond hair, and the other had black.

"My brothers." He inclined his head to them.

They inclined their heads back and went about their business of lashing the departed. Thick leather straps were whipped up, high, into the air, and they crashed down on naked flesh with a sickening *crack*. A few times, the whip came down on the same spot, leaving deep gashes pooled up with blood, quickly spilling down the bodies. The crimson fanned out by their feet, leaving the grass bloodied. I had never seen such carnage in person. The smell of blood, metallic and awful, filled my nose. The cries of those being punished reverberated back into my head, leaving me haunted by the sounds. It was, to my embarrassment, that I noticed how even the women being lashed were topless.

"This is what will happen to me?"

"Yes."

My eyes welled up with hot tears, but I blinked them back. I knew there was no escaping my punishment. It was far too late, and I had a feeling that begging would just fall on deaf ears. I had decided to take my life, though I would certainly take it back if I could. My damned soul was already ripe for the taking. Feeling so helpless just urged me to get it all over with as quickly as possible. Maybe I did deserve the punishment, after all.

The sounds were unbearable. It was a cacophony of primal screams, cries, moans, and sobs. I had never heard anything more depressing, and I wished for the silence that I took for granted. There was usually always some clamor going on. White noise, they called it. But at home, very late at night, I could achieve total quiet if I wanted it enough. In Hell, though, with the suicides, it would never be mute. The realization caused me to feel even more panic-stricken.

To try and take my mind off of the sounds, I studied each passing visage of those not currently taking punishment and peeked at their bodies: they were all dressed similarly. The men were in the same type of pants as Lucian, except theirs were hunter green. Like the men, the women had the same pants, though their tops were low-cut and ragged. The one thing each one of them had in common was a bright, bloody upside-down question mark over their hearts. *Ego Interfectum.*

"So these are only suicides, Lucian?"

"They're all classified *Animam Edere*, yes." He narrowed his eyes as he peered through the crowd.

"Then where are the murderers, and the evil world leaders, like Hitler, and those kinds of people?"

"Not in this neck of the woods."

"Can I see them?"

"No."

"Why not?"

"Because it isn't your group."

"Rules of Hell." I frowned. For sure, I thought I was going to be given the grand tour of the fiery Inferno, and not just the Woodstock of suicides. The only upside, if you had to seek optimism, was how there were no gigantic flames licking at anyone. Lucian had to know it wasn't what I had in mind.

Smug was just the way Lucian was, it appeared. After all, I hadn't known him for very long. I did know he was a being of few words, and how he had a temper problem. But he was also alluring, and could be charming. When he recounted the suicide story to me about the brother and sister, he appeared so human. Maybe a little less than human, but not just a demon straight out of Hell. He seemed to be going against the demonic stereotypes. Lucian didn't have horns, a tail, or hooves. He didn't carry a pitchfork. His skin was not red. And, yet, he was strikingly intimidating. Maybe it was just the brute force he exhibited.

"So." I glanced up at him. "Can I maybe meet your father?"

"No one *meets* him," he scoffed. "Your ignorance outweighs your disrespect—just this once."

Perhaps he had father issues. After all, the Devil—since I didn't know what he went by socially—was *Der Führer* of Hell. During my youth, I questioned both the existence of God and the Devil. I thought maybe God existed, but the Devil didn't; but, in turn, if God existed, the Devil certainly had to exist to balance things out. The same went for a belief in the Devil, but not God. And if both were just tossed aside as mere folklore, the empty void would be looming. Now I was certain there was a God, a Devil, demons, and angels. Every yin needed a yang. The scales had to weigh even on both sides. Juxtaposition.

"I don't think this is a stupid question, but—"

"It probably is."

"Is Kurt Cobain here?"

"Never heard the name."

"You remember every suicide's name?"

"Of course."

Lucian tightly grabbed onto my arm. He noticed his grasp and eased up. I could feel his tension.

"Ouch." I winced. "Shit. What?"

"There." He pointed ahead of us.

Before I had the chance to ask him about how demons

come to be, which was my burning question, I was stopped in my tracks. Sitting right in front of me, on a stone bench, were the two suicides wailing their lament to each other. They had to sit as far away as the magnet would allow, left about eight feet between them, and just not enough to make any sort of contact.

The woman was pretty, I surmised. She had thick, cold waves in her blonde hair. It was certainly twenties-chic. Her eyes were large, filled with nothing but sorrow and pain for what she had been through. Her pale, heart-shaped face matched her brother's. He, too, had large dark eyes, filled with dread and longing. My own widened as I looked between them. They kept their arms out to each other, beckoning, even though both knew they would never be able to touch. It was futile, but they wanted to overcome it.

As I was about to ask the female a question, she opened her mouth wide and let out a loud, shrill cry. I covered my ears with my hands and took a step back. Opposite her, the brother emitted the same cry.

I had no idea how I would live eternity with all of the noise.

"Please!" I shouted. "Can you just stop for a minute?"

The woman stopped, and looked at me. "What?"

"I'm just trying to, you know, get a sense of this place. I understand about the whole crying thing, but you're going to split my eardrums."

"Who are you?" She narrowed her gaze. Her brother remained silent, though his quizzical expression matched hers.

"Piper." I straightened my posture. "What's your name?"

"Pearl."

"And his?" I gestured to her brother.

"Frank."

At his sister's mention of his name, Frank buried his face in his hands. He leaned forward, though made no other movement.

"Are you staying here permanently?" Pearl wondered.

"Yes, but not just yet. Soon, though."

She wailed again; her incestuous beloved picked his head up and followed suit.

"You know," I said to Lucian, my volume cranked up, "I thought, maybe, they would at least be up for casual chit-chat with me. What, almost a century of just wailing, wailing, wailing? You'd think how they would wanna take a rest, give the vocal cords a break, and maybe have a drink of water."

Lucian laughed, baring his bright white choppers. I was stunned by the magnitude of the guffaw. And, apparently, so was everyone else. They all stopped what they were doing—even the wailers—and stared at the muscle-head. Immediately, I was nervous. I was the one who caused it. He wouldn't have laughed if it wasn't because of my little anecdote. Then again, I was feeling on top of the world for making Lucian laugh, and I didn't care about what the suicides thought. I never wanted to leave my quick wit, or sense of humor, behind, in favor of lamenting bullshit which should just be dropped and forgotten. Then again, I never had the desire to sleep with Dippy.

Another surprise had been in store for me: Lucian took my hand and clasped it. I could feel just how hot his palm was, whereas mine was ice-cold. I figured he needed to take me somewhere steep or dangerous, hence the hand-holding.

But he didn't.

Instead, Lucian took me back over to where the people were being whipped frantically and mercilessly. Their lashings were devastating; long, deep gashes across shoulders, backs, legs, and wherever else the demons saw fit. With each crack of the whip, the upside-down question marks bled and glowed red. It smelled like a butcher shop.

I was sick to my stomach, but Lucian urged me on by tugging at my hand. I wanted to tell him how I was terrified and wanted to go home now—how I had seen enough of the place where I was going to spend the rest of eternity. Right then, though, I had merely been a tourist. I didn't have to line up for a lashing, though I had something to look forward to when the dark forest became my permanent residence. Hunter green was just not a favorable color on me at all, either. My religion bound me to this travesty. If only I was raised differently.

I stopped walking, and rotated to glimpse Lucian. He appeared nervous, edgy, and slightly panicked. I never saw him completely stumble when it came to maintaining composure.

One of the suicides, a woman with long black hair, glared at me, and screamed. I thought that something was going to shatter because of her octave. Quickly, Lucian placed his hands over my ears, and I heard nothing at all. I could see her, still; she was being slashed by one of Lucian's brothers, and the other attended to someone else. I wondered what the whole deal was with loud noises—perhaps it was something of a contest.

When they finally quieted her down, Lucian removed his hands from my ears. Once again, I heard were cries of pain, begging, apologies, and insults. The shrieking woman narrowed her eyes at me and contorted her appearance into pure horror: lips curled, teeth bared, nose upturned. She was probably in her twenties when she died; she had a modern appearance, so it was probably fairly recent since she killed herself. She was snarling at me, and a low grumble in her throat metamorphosed into a full growl. She didn't seem to care that she was topless, whereas I would be mortified. I had no idea, whatsoever, what she wanted from me.

"Behave yourself," Lucian ordered. She immediately

went quiet.

"She's afraid of you," I commented.

"Yes." He nodded. "We were also intimate, previously. Not anymore."

I blanched. Was Underworld sex even allowed? Well, it had to be if Lucian had done it. And with such a psychopathic woman. But perhaps it was what he wanted in the opposite sex. I was uncertain. None of the experience made any sense to me.

She was attractive as well, with her wavy black hair, matching her onyx eyes. She sported an olive complexion. Her nose reminded me of Lucian's, narrower at the top and broader toward the bottom. Unlike me, she had full lips and a curvy body. The dark mark above her heart was bleeding profusely, but Lucian ignored it. He glared at her, eyes narrowed, and threw his arm around my shoulders. I didn't know what to do or say, or even how to react. But, apparently, this other woman did. She writhed to get out of her chains where she was being lashed, but it was a futile attempt.

One of Lucian's brothers, the blond, stepped forward and grabbed the woman tightly around the top of her arm. "Maya," he stated. "You never learn." He grinned as he quickly and forcefully brought down the whip, blow after blow, on what used to be Maya's perfect, blemish-free skin. A smile tugged at the corners of my mouth, but I bit down on my lower lip instead. Smiling at her misfortune was wrong, even though it was my gut reaction. The lashing was brutal, though; the blond was merciless, and he left canyon-sized cuts oozing blood. Not long after, Lucian's raven-haired brother joined in. He whipped her arms and legs. Maya's skin was reduced to ribbons.

When they were through, Lucian's brothers took a break. They greeted each other with some sort of odd bow-handshake, and three pairs of eyes were directed right at me.

Maya took the opportunity to run, though we all knew she wouldn't be going far. After a few moments, she collapsed onto the ground, curled up in the fetal position, and rocked back and forth. Her sobs were audible from where I had been standing, though they weren't so terrible. In a sick way, I was stoked that she was wallowing in misery. But I realized how I, too, would soon be going through the same thing.

In an effort to distract myself, I introduced myself to Lucian's kin.

"Um, I'm Piper."

One of Lucian's brothers laughed—the one who had chastised Maya. He had shoulder-length blond hair, a wide smile showing off two rows of perfectly straight teeth, though the canines were elongated, pointy, and probably sharp. He also had tattoos, though not as elegant as Lucian's. I noticed how his eyes were green, and his eyebrows were arched. He was an attractive being, undoubtedly, but

Lucian was much more my type.

"Balthazar." He washed the blood off of his hands in a nearby stream.

"Oh, like the King?"

"No." He shook his head. "This," Balthazar continued, "is our other brother, Xaphan." He gestured to the dark-haired man, standing by the river, by inclining his head to him.

Xaphan had inky black hair, shining almost-blue when he moved his head. His eyes, like Balthazar's, were green. However, Xaphan's were much more intense; they were a blue-green which were darker around the outside of the iris and got lighter as the color moved toward the pupil. Xaphan was also the shortest of the brothers; though Lucian was six-four and Balthazar was about six-one, Xaphan couldn't have been more than five-nine, at best. Still, he appeared to be the most intimidating. Maybe it was just because I was more comfortable around Lucian, but both of his brothers did scare me. They were strong-looking, though neither were bulky, which one would, perhaps, expect for the sons of the Devil.

"I remember seeing her," Xaphan, tone indifferent, stated.

"I don't remember you," I explained. "Sorry."

Balthazar laughed, though Lucian and I did not find it particularly funny. Xaphan cocked his head to the side and looked at me quizzically, as though trying to come to a decision about me. Unlike the blond, he wasn't the laughing type. His eyes revealed that he was a deep thinker, and preferred to observe rather than lend a voice.

"She has to be going," Lucian stated. He was trying to keep his tone as even as possible. I assumed his brothers were older than he was, because he was displaying enormous amounts of respect and constraint.

"So soon?" Balthazar smiled. "Maybe we can give her a taste of what's to come. What do you say, Lucian?"

Xaphan delivered the once-over to me, and a shudder moved through my body. I never thought of myself as the type of woman who needed to rely on a man to keep me safe, but I was terrified of Balthazar and Xaphan. And, sure, Lucian scared the wits out of me as well, but he wasn't the one who had a whip in his hands, ready to hand out a few lashings for shits and giggles.

"No." Lucian's tone was ice. "There's time. She'll be back soon."

So much for my knight in shining, bronze armor.

"But the fun should start right now," Balthazar insisted.

I was about to open my mouth and protest Balthazar's idea, but Lucian pressed his hand against my back, and I knew to be quiet. He knew his brothers, and if he wanted me to shut up in order to get away from them, I would.

"We have the rest of eternity," Xaphan coldly stated. He didn't say much, but when he did speak, it was pointed.

"I've got to get her along to the waiting room at the Database." Lucian clenched his fists.

Both of his brothers sneered; it was as though they were not particularly fond of this waiting room stuff Lucian was talking about. Despite not knowing exactly what he meant, Lucian promised to show me what I couldn't remember. I had already been given the tour of my eternity. The thought made me ill. In many respects, it was more like one strange, elongated dream. There was even the possibility that my brain went haywire from the lightning strike. Maybe everything had been imagined.

The three exchanged goodbyes, and Lucian was pulling me by the hand, again. I couldn't help but turn and watch Balthazar and Xaphan. Balthazar was grinning darkly, whereas Xaphan's stare pierced me. I was regretting the whole suicide attempt, and longed to be able to step back in time.

"Lucian?" I felt confident enough to speak up once we were away from his brothers.

"What?"

"This might be crossing the line, but—"

"Everything you say crosses the line, so just say it."

"How often do you, um, get involved with the suicides down here? Did you love Maya?"

Lucian stopped walking. His temples expanded and withdrew several times; I could see his jaw clench and unclench. He let go of my hand, choosing to clasp both of his behind his back as he stared straight at me. I could feel him burning a hole right through me, but I didn't back down. Instead, I looked him square in the eye and pursed my lips. Maybe I didn't have a right to know, but I was curious. Besides, he knew every little thing about me, so it was only fair.

"I'm not capable of loving." He spoke slowly and cautiously. He must have been working out choosing the right words in his mind. "So I never loved, nor do I love, Maya. She's nothing. It was purely a carnal desire."

I frowned. He had used the word carnal twice already; once to tell me how he didn't want me carnally, and the more recent to explain how he wanted Maya that way.

"So, she's your type?"

"I don't have a type. I'm not mortal, if you might remember. I'm not confined to those boxes."

"Why her?"

"She was there. Convenience."

"Is that all?" I couldn't help but feel the hot jealousy bubbling up inside of me, creeping through my veins, and making its way to my tongue, where I wanted to spit out hatred, and vile, awful insults about the both of them.

Lucian hesitated when it came to answering. He was silent for a few moments, irking me. I thought he wouldn't lie, but he needed to say things deliberately.

"It may, or may not, be all." Lucian glimpsed me suspiciously.

"What about mortals?"

"What about them?"

"Do you—you know—get involved? Sleep with them, possess them? Incubus-stuff?"

"How is this relevant to you?"

"I mean." I exhaled a long breath. "I guess, you know, it isn't. I just..."

"Oh, fantastic. Another suicide is in love with me."

"Don't flatter yourself!"

Lucian grabbed hold of my shoulders and glared down at me. I peeked up at him, and my knees buckled. My eyes welled up. I cast them downward, not wanting him to enjoy my misery.

I had never been in love. There were the crushes beyond Astronomy class, sure, but they'd never amounted to anything. I had always been too scared to tell boys how I felt about them. So, instead, I befriended them, and they'd only ever saw me as just one of the guys. They had asked me advice about girls, and told me about dates, but I was never the one who was asked out. No one had wanted to take me to dinner, or go out to see a movie which wasn't some slasher flick. I was just the girl who'd played video games, would jam on guitar, and who'd tipped extra for pizza deliveries, and always remained single. I'm sure it was a source of Dad and Dip's happiness, to not need to threaten any guys, or to feel anxiety about what time I would be walking through the door. They knew I wasn't going to get pregnant, or catch an STD. In all of my twenty-two years, I had been an utter failure with men. I would never get to remedy it.

And, to prove my true lameness, a demon rejected me.

"Why are you crying, damnit?" Lucian barked. He released me and walked again.

"I'm not crying," I said, crying. I quickened my pace to keep in line.

"Honestly," he muttered. "This is the least of your troubles. You know you're going to be tortured for the rest of eternity, and you're sobbing about how I'm not going to pin you down and have my way with you?"

I suppose he had a point. But, oftentimes, trivial matters hit the hardest. The reality of torture was still abstract to me. Sure, I had witnessed it, but it was done to others.

"No." I thought, *yes.*

"Good," he grunted. "Because you don't understand any of this."

"So, explain it to me."

"There are more important matters to attend to, believe it or not."

I knew I should loathe him. Yet, I desperately wanted him to feel the same way about me as he had once felt about Maya. I needed to know if there was more to the story. Also, I was in dire desperation to learn what act she had committed, and what led up to it in order to land her there, in Hell, with the other self-murderers.

Lucian must have thought of himself as my babysitter. The fleeting thoughts I had, about him taking an interest in me, became nothing more than dragging his proverbial kid sister around because he had to. It was his job. There was nothing more to it, despite my imagination.

No one would ever get the chance to love me. It was too late in my mortal life, and the one man I had ever feelings for thought of me as a nuisance. A job. A chore. Some awful duty he probably wished he could pass off to one of his brothers, if they weren't too busy whipping the souls of people who thought their mortal lives were just so terrible. If only they knew what was in store for them, they would have unloaded their guns, put the knives back in the drawers, closed up the pill bottles, and capped the alcohol. Maybe they would've not purchased heroin from a stranger on the street. They would have stepped back off of the ledge, kept driving over the bridge to the safety of the other side, and just worked hard at making a better life for themselves.

I should have dyed eggs with my sister.

I should have engaged Dippy in conversation.

I should have washed the dishes for my mom.

I should have gone to work with my dad.

But, more than anything, I should have gone back inside, ripped up my lists, taken the steps to get my funeral money back, and booked a trip to New Zealand for the summer. Instead, I was in Hell with a demon who I had a superficial crush on, and he didn't return the sentiment. I was sentenced to unlimited lashings, and had to listen to people scream, and wail, and bitch, forever. And, maybe, Maya would be allowed to unleash on me when I became a regular in the circle of failures.

"Lucian?"

"What now?"

"How did Maya kill herself?"

"Electric chair."

"Come again?"

Lucian appeared contemplative, as though he was weighing the idea of telling me Maya's story. His nose flared, though he did not seem as aggravated as he had just moments prior. I wondered if it was a rarity that suicides would engage the demon in conversation. He was an intimidating being, after all. But my curiosity was overwhelming, and I wanted to know as much information as my brain could possibly soak up. Everything Lucian must have seen and experienced fascinated me. Though he wasn't completely against opening up, it did take some persuasion.

"She was executed by means of the electric chair."

"So, she isn't a suicide?"

"She is," he stressed. "Because her course of actions led her to be classified as *Animam Edere*. Maya was sentenced to death after she killed her daughter."

"Jesu—"

"You can't say that here!"

"Um. Geez." I knew Denny, Abby, and I were all hand-fuls in our own right, but my mother would never physi-cally harm any of us.

"Smothered her with a pillow," Lucian continued. "And she snapped her neck for good measure, but the girl was already dead. The girl, her child, was just shy of a year old. Maya tried to plead insanity on the basis of postpar-tum depression, but it failed. In prison, she broke a mirror and sliced her wrists. The wounds were too superficial, but they were enough to have her booked here. When the jury came back with their verdict, she opted for the electric chair instead of lethal injection, figuring that the more se-verely she was punished in life, the closer she would get to redemption. Obviously, it did not work. She's been here for ten human years. Have I answered all of your burning questions about her?"

"Why did she kill her daughter?"

"Why do humans kill other humans? Selfishness."

"So she wasn't actually insane?"

"Many would argue how one must be insane to take the life of another," he stated. "But she did have her senses, if that's what you mean. She was fully aware of what she was doing. Maya believed she was too young to be a mother. To be tied down and burdened with the responsi-bility of taking care of another life for a couple of decades.

It interfered with her desires and dreams. Fame. Fortune."
Lucian wore a grimace of disapproval; his eyes narrowed
and his brows furrowed. Lucian's top lip curled up.

"You still slept with her, though," I added.

"Everyone has," he replied. "And she means nothing
to any of us. None of them do."

"Oh." Lucian's words punched me in the guts. I didn't
want to be filed away as just another suicide statistic.

I needed a way out. I needed a miracle.

15

Quota

THE PLACE I WAS TAKEN to was a far walk from the forest of suicides. My demonic guide never broke his stride, so I ended up lagging behind. I tried to keep up with his steps as we climbed over grassy hills. Though his expression was blank, I figured he was enjoying it.

"Lucian?"

His jaw clenched; I could see his temples flaring in and out, again.

"What?"

"Remember when you told me how I was yours? My soul, I mean. When you pulled me onto your lap and all?"

"Yes."

"Well what exactly did you mean by it? Because when we got down here, it was like a free-for-all, you know?" I tried to keep my voice as even as possible. Lucian did seem to hold claim to me. If it meant falling under his protection, I would at least feel somewhat better.

"It means…" He stopped in his tracks so I could catch up. "Your soul goes into my quota. I claim it because I'm the one who will take it from you. Not Balthazar or Xaphan."

I pursed my lips at how straightforward and blunt he was. Of course he wouldn't exercise the same sort of compassion and sympathy other people did—because he wasn't a human. He was a demon and proving it with each heart-shattering word he said. I had to accept that I wasn't special at all. My soul didn't appeal to him any more than the other thousands of souls that entered his realm via suicide.

"So the quota thing is Hell's dick-measuring contest."

Lucian sighed. "Humans. Such eloquence."

"We're not so awful."

"Let me guess," Lucian smirked. "You thought I might see you as something more than just another life-waster."

"Yes," I honestly replied.

He looked at the ground. "You aren't."

"I could have been."

"Could have. Would have. Should have." Lucian met my gaze, again. "You all say the same trite, passive phrases."

His words zapped my nerves. For a moment, all I could do was stand there, stunned. Nothing got sugar-coated by a demon.

I peered out on the horizon, watching as the black sky swirled into a deep, rich navy blue. The stars got a bit duller but I was glad to be away from the darkness, even if it would only be for a short period of time. The area around us was what I would liken to a forest clearing. There were a few trees scattered around; I saw a stream, and plenty of grass, though no flowers.

I moved my fingers through my hair, and inhaled the scent around us. It was akin to nature, though with super-natural elements added to it. The smell of incense still en-twined with the natural air, giving each gentle breeze a sweet, intoxicating smell. I was just contented to get far away from the screaming suicides, and to be in a place where the only noises I could hear were my breathing, Lu-cian's, and the soft lullaby of the mild wind.

Lucian directed me through a tall, elegant bronze gate with intricate swirls. The man standing beside it curtly nodded at my companion, though no words were ex-changed between the two. I kept quiet and fixed my view on the ground until we were several yards away from the gatekeeper.

The sky was even lighter; a rich, cornflower blue. The stars served as soft, twinkling lights to further illuminate the sky. Where we were walking, the smell of incense got less and less potent, though something else took its place: Freesia.

"This doesn't feel like Hell at all," I murmured.

"Because it isn't," Lucian explained.

"Then what is it?"

"Purgatory."

I passed the gate of Hell and entered the gate of Purgatory like it was a cakewalk. I wondered where the dark creatures that were supposed to come out and guard the place were hiding, but decided against asking Lucian.

"Lucian?"

"No one has ever talked to me this much—combined."

"Oh." I peeked down at my shoes.

"Just ask."

"Well. You know all the details about me, don't you?"

"Yes; I suppose I do."

"So maybe you can tell me just a little bit about you. I mean, I'm going to be hanging around a lot, aren't I? It can't be so awful if we just got acquainted. More than you just appearing from nowhere and letting me see all of your tattoos." I bit down on my lip, attempting to conceal my smile. I had no reason, whatsoever, to smile, but I couldn't stop myself.

"You're grinning like a fool," he assessed. "They all do."

"What do you mean?"

"The suicides. They're drawn to us. Enchanted by us, if you will. Think of it the way—ah, how do you Americans use the metaphor—like butterflies to sugar." He looked down at me and I met his stare; immediately I was weakened.

"Thought you were going to say flies to shit," I quipped.

"No."

"Ok, well, tell me more about it. Tell me why I feel like this. What did you call it? Enchanted?"

"There's nothing special about the way it works. We have the power over you and you're drawn to it because we could benefit you—even if the chance is less-than-zero. You all have—"

"Hope," I concluded.

"Hope. What a disgusting word."

"So we're naturally drawn to you. It isn't because of the way you act or look—"

"Well, obviously, those factor in as well."

"Oh, obviously."

"I'm through talking about this," Lucian stated.

"A few more questions, come on. I really want to know—"

"No."

Silence fell between us as we took a few more steps forward. The scent of Freesia was becoming more potent as the incense died away. I was relieved to see the sky above us lightening even further into a rich cerulean. It filled me, just a little bit, with the word Lucian hated so much: hope. I didn't have it about much, but I did have it about the sky. If only the sky could open up. A line from a movie said something so awe-inspiring about such an event.

"If the sky were to suddenly open up, there would be no law, there would be no rule. There would only be you and your memories."

"What?"

"It's just this movie I saw a few years ago–"

"Fascinating." The sarcasm rolled off of the demon's tongue.

"Which of you is the oldest?" I carefully chose my inquiry. "There. A reasonable question."

"Xaphan is," he said after a pause. "And then me, and then Balthazar."

"So three brothers..."

"Three full brothers."

"Oh." I thought about it for a moment. Surely there had to be more demons running around. It was strange to me how the brothers didn't have many physical comparisons, except for certain shared traits. Lucian was above and beyond the other two in the looks department. "And it's their job to punish the suicides?"

"Partly."

"Do you get a lot of cases like me?"

"You've been the most... challenging."

"Why?"

I could see his nostrils flare, and his intense blue eyes blazed. It appeared as though he was elevated, but it just had to be my imagination. He was an intimidating being—so tall, with pure muscle mass and a terrifying stare. He was hardened to the nth degree.

His silence told me how he didn't want to answer my question. A hundred thoughts flooded through my head, though most of them had to do with the sliver of possibility he might care for me in some capacity, and didn't actually want to send me to his brothers to get brutally punished.

"Oh come on, Lucian," I whined. "Answer my question."

"You ask far too many questions."

"Just tell me what makes me different."

Lucian sighed and raked his fingers over his buzz of hair. I still couldn't tell what the hesitation was on his part but it was making me feel anxious. If there was something I could possibly have an upper-hand about, I would utilize it.

"Aside from your constant need to speak, and ask questions, and engage me in conversation... you have angels."

Angels. Arella and Hael. Of course. But they had no

way of helping me out. I mocked them, and didn't believe what they told me. And, now, it was far too late to do anything about it. I was sure that angels couldn't just fly right down into Purgatory, scoop up their human, and fly her away to safety. There was no phone line from where I was to anywhere else. It was me and Lucian.

"Not everyone has angels?"

"No." He shook his head. "Angels are complicated. They have intricate rules about their loyalties, though I'm not privy to that information—before you ask."

"Oh," I managed to croak out. "I offended them. I don't think they even care about me, anymore."

Lucian narrowed his eyes at me, most likely not believing what I had just told him. But my own was free of guilt, and I saw how he noticed it.

He desperately wanted to drop the issue, so I got quiet for a few moments in order to think. If only it had been possible to make an escape. Where I was, though; and, more importantly, who I was with, was an indicator that I wasn't going anywhere. Lucian would not let me out of his sight. I was part of his important quota he had to fill. Perhaps it was why he wouldn't let his brothers near me. If anything happened to me, since I was still in human form, some sort of law could have been breached, and Lucian wouldn't get to claim me.

And I actually thought he would have saved me.

My mother always told me to never rely on a man to

get what you want and need. That a woman is more than capable of doing what was necessary in order to make a better life for herself. My mother was also a hypocrite and leeched off of my father for every dime he labored for.

"Where are we going?" I knew I acted like a child. I might as well just have been hanging off of him and yelling, "Are we there yet?" into his pointy ear.

"How many times do I have to tell you?" He was obviously angry about what had already unfolded.

"I know. But where is it located? Far from here?"

"Not far. As soon as the sky turns the actual color of the sky. Azure."

I continued walking. There were so many questions I wanted to ask Lucian, but was too scared to bother him with any of them. I wanted to know if he was still collecting souls, or if they were on hold because of me. Maya, and her whole situation, was still at the forefront of my mind, but I kept trying to push it back. Xaphan and Balthazar's stories intrigued me almost as much as Lucian's. A round of twenty-one questions would have been wonderful, but I knew what his answer would be, anyway.

"How did you come to be?" I finally summoned the courage to ask my burning question.

Lucian stopped dead in his tracks, and I bumped into him from behind. He pivoted around.

"Look." Lucian frowned. "Go into the building right there." He ignored my query, and pointed to a white city-hall type of building, surrounded by gorgeous fountains, large marble steps, and greenery. It was lovely.

"You're not coming with me?" A lump formed at the base of my throat.

"I'm not allowed inside," Lucian explained. "Enter through the main doors, walk up to the front desk, and give them your name. They're going to give you an hour to view your records, so I'll meet you right here—and you better be here—in one hour from when you step inside." Lucian nudged me.

I pursed my lips at him.

"Go."

"Okay, okay."

I walked toward the white building, thinking about my family as I did so. No time would be lapsing for them whatsoever. It was so strange to think about. I wondered how much had happened in this realm when I was sleeping through the night, or when I was brushing my teeth. Months could have passed down here. One brush stroke could have been an entire week.

I got closer and closer to the building with each step. I placed my hands on the door and pushed it open, stepping inside.

16

DMV

THE INTERIOR OF THE building reminded me of the old courthouses my family and I once visited when we went to historic Williamsburg in Virginia, combined with a DMV. The furnishings were immaculate and polished to perfection. I didn't know what to expect when I walked in, but was pleasantly surprised to find how it wasn't all doom and gloom. There was a desk directly in front of me, with a line of about a dozen people standing in front of it. All of the furniture was comprised of wood; high-gloss mahogany, completely free of any smudges or dust.

Beyond the desk was a semi-circle of stools curving

around one large expanse of desk area. Occupying the empty space between were rows and rows of benches, like church pews. There must have been a hundred people in the room, not counting those who were on line in front of me. Some of them were stretched out, completely, on the benches. Others took to sitting around the floor, or just walking around the place, admiring the various pieces of furniture, all leather-bound and expensive.

One of the more odd things I had noticed was how there were no clocks or any sense of time. I didn't know if I would make it out of there in an hour or not, causing me to panic. Lucian wasn't the type who waited around for people, especially when he had given such a specific length of time. One hour. Surely he had taken the line into consideration, though. Even if he hadn't ever been in there, he must have been aware that swarms of souls go in there to get whatever it was they need.

The people in line were all different; I saw elderly folks, twenty-somethings, middle-aged men and women, and a solitary teenager. I noticed they were all deadly serious and frightened. I shared their apprehension.

As I waited in line, I thought about my family. How they had no idea how I was going through any of this. Dippy came to my thoughts immediately. Given the newfound information I had acquired, it scared me to think he had almost—or actually—died. It was probable that he had been in the same place where I was standing. But he probably recalled none of it.

When my turn came up, I stepped forward and cleared my throat. The woman behind the desk was pale, but her skin was radiant. She had platinum blonde hair, cropped into a short bob with accompanying bangs, cut above her sharply arched, dark eyebrows. Her eyes were a dark violet; they immediately drew me in. Her nametag, tacked onto a crisp, white, button-down shirt, read *Shayle*. Because she was sitting down, I could not see the rest of her. I did notice, though, how she was polite enough to smile. Her smile revealed bright white, perfectly straight teeth. Above her Cheshire grin was a small, straight nose pointed upward at the tip.

She was so lovely. So tiny as well; I couldn't imagine Shayle being more than five feet tall.

"Hi," I managed to say, though my voice was a bit high—probably due to nerves.

"Hello," she replied. "And your business?"

"Sorry?"

"Natural death, murder, accident," Shayle quickly explained. "Via home, auto, accidental overdose. Or, suicide." I couldn't help but notice how her nails were painted the same color of her eyes.

"I was—I am—a suicide. But that's—"

"Suicides take the red ticket." She motioned to a machine in the center of a table off to the side. It fed pieces of paper with numbers on them, so you would know when it was your turn.

"The thing is, ah, Shayle, I'm here because I need to know about—"

"Suicide," she stated once again. "Take the red ticket, please and thank you!"

I frowned.

Why didn't people listen, anymore?

I meandered over to the ticket machine and pushed the 'Suicide' button. A piece of white paper, with a red letter, and numbers, shot out of it.

"S471," I read aloud. I slid down onto one of the benches, feeling relieved that the bench part was covered with a lovely, thick, green leather cushion.

It wasn't like a regular DMV, where people got completely aggravated. It wasn't a decrepit mess, either; in fact, it was clean and tidy, with a floral scent wafting through the air. The source was not too far away—I saw a large vase of roses beside Shayle, though she paid no mind to them. They were blood-red roses, mixed in with a few black. It had to be a gift from a demon, as opposed to an angel. I assumed that angels sent things like white roses and baby's breath. Maybe an array of carnations.

I had to stop gawking at Shayle, though I found it nearly impossible. The way I gaped at Lucian was the way I stared at her. She was just so intriguing. I wondered if she was an angel; surely, she could not be a demon, but anything was possible.

The overhead ticket display had been calling N411, N412, and N413, all with a combination of M280, M281, M282. There were also A903, A904, A905, and one S470.

It wasn't too hectic, I figured. So I sat down and held my ticket in my hand, feeling on edge. Deep down, I just wanted to go home and change the past. Make sure Denny never went off to serve in the war. He would work in building a closer relationship to Abigail, so she wouldn't be such a difficult little brat. And it would leave more alone time for Mom and Dad to work out their issues. As long as my family was healthy and not broken, I thought I would have a chance. As it turned out, though, it wasn't what had happened.

I did start to feel iffy about leaving them. It wasn't like I did nothing for them. I was always around to keep my brother company when he was sad about the war, and about his missing leg, and about not being able to do anything anymore, which is why all he did was drugs. Maybe Abigail would have listened, and followed me, if I switched off the television and took her out to teach her some of my favorite things: how to draw and make origami. When we were done playing, we could help our mother out with the house responsibilities. It wasn't as though I went to school everyday. My classes were only three times a week, for a few hours at a time. When I did have free time, and wasn't working, I could have been doing so much more. Instead, time was wasted in a concentrated effort to be lazy, depressed, and self-loathing.

And all it took for it to dawn on me was my death. My suicide.

With a *ding* of the overhead bell, I glanced at the numbers and sighed. Not mine.

To the right of me were A905, A904, and A903. They sat there, stunned. I knew the feeling.

"Hey. Hi," I waved. The group consisted of two men and a young woman. I figured she didn't think anyone would speak to her, but I wanted to get as much information as I possibly could from the woman who had long, thick red hair that went to her waist.

"Hello... or maybe good afternoon, I guess," she finally said. I noticed her eyes were hazel green. "Or good morning, or good evening. I just don't know."

American accent—slightly Midwestern.

"What happened? If you don't mind my asking."

"Well, I was driving on the road when this one—" she pointed to the man on one side of her, "Tailgated me. And that one—" she said, pointing to the other man, who was keeping his head low, "was in front of me."

The woman took a deep breath and raked her fingers through her hair. I was familiar with the process. She appeared to be in her mid-thirties, as did the other gentlemen. One had ash-brown hair and light brown eyes, and the other, with his head lowered, had black hair. I couldn't see his eyes, as he refused to glance up.

"Anyway," the woman continued. "I stopped because I hate tailgaters. Figured I'd get a little bump to the back of the car and then the guy would owe me a new paint job, you know? But that never happened."

"How come?"

"Because the moron came barreling down at me! Hit me hard from the rear, and I lost control of my car, and went right into his in front of me." She struggled to keep talking, but was able to brazen through. "His car," she pointed to the black-haired guy. "Was hit pretty badly. On top of that, he lost control of the vehicle, tried to get his wheel straight, but couldn't. He ended up upside-down in a ditch. Car landed upside-down and he broke his neck. Dead instantly. He says he had been going home from working extra hours."

My oculars filled up with the salty stuff as I glanced at the black-haired gentleman, who was innocent in all of this. He glanced up, just for a moment, so I mouthed a "sorry" to him. I had a positive feeling that I knew where he was going. But his life was still taken away from him.

"And so how did you two die?" I wondered.

The rear-ender ignored me, but the other man lifted his head up, keeping it there, to look at me. Meanwhile, the woman kept answering my questions.

"We both got out of our cars and screamed at each other, causing a whole bunch of commotion. I know that the both of us had hit our heads pretty hard on the airbags, so we were staggering around, trying to shove each other and place blame. Except we were just so out of it that I swayed, grabbed onto his shirt, and we both went tumbling right down on top of his car. Can you believe that? I snapped my neck, and then I was suddenly standing there, watching everything. I thought that this other guy, here, was going to make it, but then the car burst into flames before that could happen. Isn't that a bitch?"

I didn't know what emotion to show—a jaw drop, an eye pop, a deep stare. It was one of the craziest road stories I had ever heard, though it was probably because I knew where they had ended up because of it. The Purgatory Department of Deaths.

"It is a bitch," I nodded. "How'd you get here?"

"A woman picked us up."

"Who?"

"I don't know. She didn't say much."

"They have a tendency to not say much, it seems."

"What's your name?" The redhead asked.

"Oh, I'm Piper. Piper Marino. And you are?"

"Liz," she said. "Elizabeth Delray, but just call me Liz."

I smiled at Liz, hoping she would get a less severe punishment. She wasn't a murderer. It was all an accident. My eyes flicked over to the two men. The one with the black hair appeared ashen and terrified. I thought, for sure, he was going to vomit.

"What are you in here for, Piper?" Liz said.

"I'm a complicated suicide searching for an answer about when I died. They're going to take my soul and send me to Hell soon, and I need my answers before I can do that." I hoped the woman, Liz, would get the gist of what I was trying to say. I resorted to speaking Underworld.

"Wow." She shook her head. "Good luck, honey."

"Thanks."

"Piper." The man with the dark hair and blue eyes was talking to me. I cocked my head to the side. His voice was familiar.

"Yes?"

"Piper who knows that my favorite ice cream is rocky road. In a waffle cone. Piper who I've been praying for each and every night with my children? Piper... the suicide girl."

Nothing could have prepared me.

"Jerry?"

"Yes."

I broke down in an instant. Jerry was dead. Jerry, a decent man with a helpful job and a loving family. Jerry the suicide hotline chatter, there to make sure no one died if he could help it. I felt such guilt, such anguish. My insides were squirming, and I itched to peel out of my skin and transform into someone else.

"Oh, Jerry, I'm so sorry." I wrapped my arms around

him and cried, muttering apologies. I was sorry for it all.

Jerry wrapped his arms back around me, and I could feel his chest heaving from crying, too. I knew he was going to get a lovely afterlife. He was an innocent victim and would be sent straight to Heaven—if it was any consolation to what he had gone through and who he had left behind.

"Piper, I wish you hadn't done that," Jerry sniffed. "And look how pretty you are, too."

He looked at me as though I still had a world of potential inside of me, even though I didn't. I was doomed to repeat the same routine for eternity. Pain and misery was just around the corner, but I had some sense of peace knowing that the man who was so helpful in life was going to be rewarded for it. My punishment suited my crime. I had taken life for granted, and now I was going to pay for it.

"I know, Jerry. I know. I regret it now, honest. But I sealed my fate already." I forced myself to smile for him. "But, hey, I know you're going straight up there. Pearly gates and all. Put in a good word for me, all right?"

Jerry nodded. His eye juice was leaking all down his reddened cheeks. "My kids…"

"They were so lucky to have you as a parent," I consoled.

"What did I do wrong?" Jerry pleaded.

"Nothing. Not one thing."

For a fleeting moment, I wondered if maybe Jerry was killed by association, because of me. *No*, I thought. *Life can't be so unjust.* Jerry had been right when he told me how life was what we made of it. How misery is a choice, and how we could pull ourselves out of it if we had the desire. But Jerry never chose misery, and his life was cut short.

"Jerry." I hugged him tighter. "Remember the last time we spoke? You—you wanted to tell me something. What was it?"

The man with the one-way ticket to Heaven pulled away, just a fraction, and glanced down into my eyes. His were bright blue; warm, sad, and worried.

"I wanted to tell you that I was like you, once."

My knees became weakened. Jerry sat me down and took a seat beside me.

"You tried to kill yourself?" I was scared for him; this new information could put his soul in jeopardy, and I did not want that for him. For someone so loving and helpful.

"No. I was too scared to try. But I thought about it a lot. I wanted to tell you, I understand. I know the desperation. I didn't feel, I don't know, right, telling you during our first conversation. We're supposed to keep it positive."

I felt a weight lift from my already-heavy shoulders. He would get salvation.

"Forgive me?" He pleaded.

"What for?"

"For not telling you."

I shook my head. "There's nothing to be sorry about. This would have happened, regardless. You can influence someone so much, but only they can make the final decision. Mine wouldn't have changed. But if you need it, you've got my full forgiveness, and so much more. Eternal gratitude."

"I was just doing my job," he shrugged.

"You went above-and-beyond," I insisted. "Honest."

My number lit up on the screen.

"Enjoy Nirvana, Jerry. My number's up." We hugged goodbye. I enjoyed the warmth radiating off of him.

"Be good," he told me. "Please."

"For you, anything."

I made my way to station number four, on the far left of the semi-circle. I placed my ticket down onto the counter, and politely smiled to the older gentleman behind the desk. He spoke before I was able to.

"Oh, dear. Yes. Suicide." He furrowed his brow. The man, whose nametag read, *Foster*, was a bit too curt for my taste. And I always thought how the English were supposed to be overly polite.

"Yeah. Suicide. Yeah."

"Your information, please."

"Well my name's Piper Angela Lily Marino. Born in Freedom Island, New York, on the thirtieth of July, nineteen eighty-six. Date of Death, uh… well, technically, I guess—"

"You guess?" His big, blue eyes narrowed in confusion. Maybe he hated his job, and it was made even worse because of ignorant people like me.

"See, I'm not, you know, technically dead. My soul and body are one. I died, temporarily, which is why I'm here. I was told I could see what went on during all of it, and then I have to be taken back up to above ground to… um, to set everything back in motion, I guess."

Foster stared at me. He appeared to be about fifty to fifty-five. His forehead was lined with wrinkles; and, his hair, cropped short, was salt-and-pepper. Foster spoke with a dignified English accent.

"Lucian sent you."

"Yes."

Foster nodded curtly, and shuffled around with papers for a moment. His palms seemed clammy. He walked around to the doors of the elongated semi-circle desk and pushed through, beckoning me to follow.

"Right," he said. "Here is a copy of your file. You'll find what you need right in there. This is the key." Foster handed me a highly-polished, gold skeleton key. It weighed about a pound.

I held onto everything he handed to me, and he escorted me into a hallway, secluded from the rest of the place. There were three doors; one straight ahead, one to the left, and one to the right.

"The key I provided you with is for the left door. Go in there, lock the door behind you, open your envelope, read the instructions, and carry them out, precisely. Any questions, Piper?"

I gaped at him. He was just so professional, and knew exactly what he was doing, whereas I was just confused, and wished my mind was clear.

"Will it hurt?"

"No." Foster chuckled. "It will not hurt, I can promise."

"Am I going to have to come back here after I die for real next time?"

"I'm afraid so." Foster patted me on the shoulder.

It wasn't the most comforting of gestures, but it was appreciated nonetheless; besides, it had a familiarity. I could have gone for a bear hug, but no one close to me was down in the Underworld with me. I was utterly alone.

"Okay," I nodded.

"Piper." Foster inched closer. "Please come directly to me when you do come back. No ticket. Just come to number four; I'm always there."

"Thanks, Foster. You're making this whole horrible thing a little more tolerable."

And I got what I had wanted: an embrace. Foster hugged me, and I hugged back. It was not awkward, nor was it comforting. But it was enough to make contact on a somewhat human level. It meant a lot to me, to embrace and form a connection. He pulled away a few moments later, and I put my head down, immediately, not wanting to show him my tear-stained profile. Crying was tolerable when I was alone, and had no one to watch me spew my emotions.

"It'll be all right, Piper," he urged. He gently guided me to the door.

"See you soon, Foster."

"Best of luck."

I opened the next door of my journey.

17

Middle Door

THE ROOM WAS SMALL, and had minimal furniture; white paint, white tiled floor, and four walls, about five feet wide on each; there was also a desk, chair, and two doors. One door I came in through, and, the other, on the exact opposite side, was a mystery. I did what Foster told me, though. After I closed the door behind me, I rotated the lock until it clicked into place. No one could enter. I nervously shuffled over to the chair and sat down, feeling pleasantly surprised at how comfortable it was. The chair was reminiscent of a computer one, except in all white, with a white leather cushion. They kept the room slightly cool, which was a relief. With the envelope firmly held between my fingers, I tried to keep my thoughts positive. It was difficult to not think of my family at a time like that, though. How nothing had changed for them since I left. I found that time was a funny thing.

I decided it would be better to just get it over with quickly, the way someone with courage would rip off a Band-Aid. My fingers slid along the flap and I emptied the contents of the envelope onto the desk.

A key, similar to the one I used to enter the room, clunked out onto the tabletop. It was bright silver, and roughly the same size as the gold key Foster gave me. A slip of white paper slid out of the envelope when I tipped it upside down, shaking it to check for other contents.

There were only two words printed on the note:

Middle Door

I thought, *Simple enough.* But the host of butterflies living in my stomach violently fluttered their wings. With each step I took, I was working toward sealing my fate. I would never see my parents or my siblings again. Instead, I was doomed to party like it was thirteen fifty-nine.

There was nothing I could do, though. Lucian allowed me one hour and he was capable of doing things I couldn't even imagine.

Plucking up the small shreds of courage I possessed, I took the heavy silver key in hand and walked to the middle door. My hand trembled, and a bead of sweat dripped from my brow onto my cheek as I pushed the key in and rotated it to the right. There was the distinct *click* of a door opening, and the handle eased and revolved.

I walked through the door as it opened of its own accord and was surrounded, momentarily, by whiteness. The floor was completely solid, but appeared to be covered in liquid nitrogen. When the mist cleared, I was able to see my surroundings. The room was a one-seat movie theater, minus the concessions. I was kind of excited to see the large silver screen flush against the wall. After walking up the stairs to get to the seat, I plopped myself into it. The chair was extra-wide, and firm enough to hold me up, but it did feel squishy; it reminded me of the leather chair my parents put in Denny's room.

Once I was in my seat, all of the lights went out and the screen took on a life of its own. The illumination was brilliantly bright and shining. Numbers from four to one flashed, real old-fashioned, on it.

And then I saw myself lying in a hospital bed. My eyes were closed.

"Good Lord, why weren't we told she was gonna be doing something like this, Momma? I can't believe that Lu—"

"I don't know what in the world she was thinking, but I *know* that she's gonna get written up for this. I'm so mad; I can't believe it came to this."

Hael and Arella were on the left side of my unconscious body, except they had appeared completely different. They'd been glowing, and they had halos and colossal, feathery, white wings. As I watched, I was anxious when Hael had tried to mention someone, but Arella cut her off. I couldn't help but wonder if my life had been written somewhere before I was born. Mapped out.

"So what should we do?" Hael had wondered.

"Pray," Arella answered.

The two angels had hovered over me; heads bowed, and hands clasped together in prayer. I couldn't decipher what they'd been saying; they had been speaking in Tongues, and their voices had raised higher, rising to the Heavens like the sound of bells chiming. It was divine.

"She ain't here," Arella'd stated. Her eyes went deer-in-headlights.

"Where is she?"

The video crinkled and appeared grainy after a moment of television static. Snow.

I'd been standing at the gate of Purgatory, with a piece of paper in my hand. I watched myself looking at it, but I couldn't see it, because the screen only showed a landscape and did not zoom in on anything. For the life of me, as I sat there watching, I could not recall what was in the letter. But I walked on after the man at the gate had written something on the slip of paper.

The direction I'd walked to was the same exact one

Lucian and I took together to get to the Database. I watched myself nervously eyeing the place, my arms curled around my body.

I'd been in the stupid hospital gown, except it was clean and did not have a rip in it. Dead-Me had staggered around the area for a few moments, stupidly confused and crying these giant, fat, swelled tears. It was, by far, the most fucked-up home video I ever saw. Maybe if I had a bucket of popcorn and some M&Ms, it would have been a better experience for me. Then again, I was watching a video of myself, walking into doom, and I couldn't do a thing about it.

Dead-Me had meandered around a few gardens, marveling at the sunflowers, and patches of pansies, before finally stepping inside the large white building. She'd taken her position in line and watched, in what I can only describe as total mind-numbness, as the queue moved forward. To my delight, Shayle hadn't been behind the counter, though some sort of opposite Shayle was. It was perplexing to see. The woman had midnight-black hair in a blunt bob with bangs, and pale lilac eyes—so pale, in fact, that they were almost white. It had an intense impact against her olive-colored skin. She'd worn the same clothes as the previous customer assistant, though her nametag read *Talia*. Also, like her counterpart, she had incredibly white teeth, though Talia's appeared to be sharper; they also had the same appearance in height.

Dead-Me had gone up to her, dejected, and sniffled. "This big, angry guy sent me here," she'd explained to Talia.

Talia took the slip from Dead-Me's hands and looked it over.

"I told him, time and time again, not to let anyone through without an escort, and I don't see any escort here. Honestly! His brothers follow the rules, but he's incapable..." She'd banged a rubber stamp down on it before scribbling something. "You have to fill these out," she continued. "In the meantime, go get a red ticket. There's a long line today so by the time you finish filling those out, you'll probably be called shortly thereafter."

Dead-Me nodded. She'd been given a clipboard, and a thick stack of papers to fill out. I peeked down at my left hand and winced, thinking about all of the writing I had to do.

Watching someone fill out forms is not the most exciting thing in the world. Sure, sometimes it can fun when they include you by ticking off a whole list of different, odd diseases no one had ever heard of, and certainly couldn't pronounce.

IT WAS DURING ONE of the meetings for families affected by the war when I had learned about trichotillomania. Sometimes, they'd said, soldiers would come home with a whole laundry list of these mental disorders. Post Traumatic Stress Disorder, or PTSD as it was referred to, was the most common. It was also the one Dippy had.

He had put a check next to all of the following symptoms on his medical sheet after he got back.

Nightmares.

Flashbacks.

Actually being back in the place of trauma.

Scary thoughts you cannot control.

Feeling worried.

Guilty.

Sad.

Alone.

Angry.

Always tired.

Suicidal.

Dippy had never liked sharing his war stories, insisting how there was nothing worth talking about. He often became withdrawn, and would isolate himself for extended periods of time, only allowing me, or Abby, to bring him food in the basement two times a day. It went on for weeks until he had an old friend over—a girl—and they spent the night together. I never knew what she did, exactly, but Dippy went back upstairs for breakfast. He sat down and helped me and Abigail with our homework assignments. Slowly, he had begun to form some resemblance of my older brother.

The suicidal check on Dip's sheet worried me, but

when I saw it, he told me how he was only joking about it. I couldn't tell, though. He seemed to desire the peace and quiet of death. If he only knew.

Even the family members of veterans—dead or alive, wounded or alive, or a psychological mess and alive—developed some of these disorders. Not many were as deep as PTSD, but there had been a woman there, about thirty-five years old, hunched over a metal folding chair. Her silent sobs shook her skinny body up and down, but no one was making much of a fuss about it. It was my first time there, and I was too scared to go over to her, fearing she would snap at me and try to bite my hand off if I'd placed it on her shoulder.

But she switched gears. She lifted up her arm, dropped her hand down onto her head, let her fingers fork through it, and tugged—hard. Already I could see a few bald patches and the remainder of hair was orange, frazzled, and clumped together by natural hair oil, meaning she hadn't washed it in a long time.

I'd nudged my mom in the ribs, but she had hissed at me to not make a fool of the family.

The lady, a deceased sergeant's wife from what Dippy told us, had tugged and tugged until she released a guttural scream and moved her hand away, where a clump of dead copper strands lay. She'd taken a break from her activity and went back to the original one: sobbing.

Dead-Me filled out all of her forms, and, not a moment later, got up from where she'd been sitting. Her number had been called, so she'd wandered over to Foster and had a seat.

The sly devil. He should have told me how he already knew who I was—how we had already met. After all, it wasn't like he was breaking some sort of confidentiality clause, since I was the same patient.

Nevertheless, the man clearly had his reasons. I probably wouldn't have believed him; but, then again, I had seen a lot of things, already, that I would have never believed.

Dead-Me and Foster had sat across from each other, the former sobbing into a tissue after it had given to her by the latter.

"What a stupid thing to do," Dead-Me sobbed.

"We do tend to hear that often," Foster quipped.

"Can I get my life back?"

"Well, that depends on a few things, really. If your spirit guide and guardian angels can get a waiver for life, then yes."

"But that's fan-fucking-tastic news!" Dead-Me shouted.

Foster had nearly fallen back in his seat.

"Erm, yes, but it may not happen. Also, you are…" Foster had trailed off, thumbing through the seemingly endless bundles of loose paper, until he'd come upon an egg-shell white form. "Right," he murmured, "I see here that you're a Catholic. Oh, dear."

"What does 'oh, dear' mean?" Dead-Me demanded. "Is that bad?"

"Well," replied Foster, "Er, suicides, as in the case of yourself, being Catholic and active—well not too active, but active enough for sacraments and things of that nature—erm..."

"Please just say it."

"Your soul has been condemned. You're to spend eternity in Hell when you do, in fact, actually cross over. Your life is up in the air right now, so we don't know, exactly, if you'll be staying here for a long time or a short time. Though the latter will either mean that you die and go off to Hell, or resume living—in which you will not remember any of this bit right here. But, yes, and then when you do die in that life, you will be back here again. Sorry."

Dead-Me gaped at Foster. She'd been just as confused as I was. The poor thing. She sobbed again, and Foster had appeared utterly bewildered. Though he had probably been through it plenty of times, he still appeared horrified by the crying.

"Please," he'd begged. "Please don't cry, Piper. Remain positive."

"What's there to be positive about?" I sobbed.

The door had banged open.

There was Lucian, red and steaming. He'd stomped into the room, teeth bared, and he sneered at Foster.

"You're not allowed in here!" Foster had boldly stated.

Talia jumped up from her chair. Some of the other workers seemed terrified, as others took bemused interest. Dead-Me stared, dumbfounded, at the demon.

"Be quiet." Lucian had growled, ignoring the rules.

"You're breaking the law," Foster continued. Lucian's huge arm had darted out like a viper; his hand seized Foster's throat.

"Hey!" Dead-Me had shouted.

Lucian whipped his gaze at me. "You have some nerve, Suicide."

"Not more than you do. Let him go!"

"The angels," Talia'd hissed. "Lucian!"

The demon had snapped out of his crazed daze and released Foster from his grasp. Dead-Me'd frowned, her arms folded across her chest. It had brought her out of her apathy.

"Sir." Foster'd coughed. "I thought, perhaps, Ms. Marino here ought to stay, at the very least, overnight. We need to have a quick chat with her spiritual mentors, and see what the prognosis is over on the other side. Protocol, you understand—ah, sir."

Poor Foster.

Lucian had fixed his eyes on Dead-Me, and I saw the faintest hint of a smile. I could see something in his eyes. They'd danced; flickering fire had been moving around his pupils.

Dead-Me had stared up into them, and her jaw had gone slack. She'd let her arms fall back into place, and she hadn't appeared angry, anymore.

"It always works." Lucian had chuckled and extended his hand to stroke Dead-Me's hair. "Send a message to me within the hour." Lucian released my hair from his grasp and walked back out, a few stares following him.

"I'll have to call security next time," Foster'd insisted.

"That's the guy who dragged me to the big, bronze gate," I'd noted. "Then he shoved me through. Didn't even answer any of my questions."

"Yes."

"Who, exactly, is he, Foster?"

"You don't want to really know. Not yet."

He was right.

CRACKLE OF STATIC-SNOW.

Dead-Me had been walking toward the door on the right, holding a lead key in her hand. Foster had his hand on her back, and he was guiding her along, smiley and cheery. He'd bent to whisper something in her ear, and she appeared to smile, though it could have been just a flicker.

Dead-Me had opened the door and stepped forward.

Crackle of static-snow.

"She's comin' around, Momma," Hael had said in hushed tones.

A bright light to the side of Hael flashed, and it had vanished a second later.

"Never stays too long." Arella shook her head.

"I'll go alert the family, and then fill out that paperwork."

"Good."

"Momma?"

"Yeah?"

"Never mind."

Hael had hurried off and slipped out of the room as Arella'd drawn closer to Dead-Me, whose finger twitched. Slowly, she'd opened her eyes and blinked at Arella.

"Piper Marino." She'd smiled. "Welcome back."

THE SCREEN WENT DARK, dull, and lifeless. It took a few moments for me to get out of the seat, but I managed. Despite my body feeling completely numb, I found my way back into the small, white room. I stuffed the essentials back into the envelope, and exited, closing the door behind me.

Foster was there to greet me. I contemplated yelling at him for not say anything about already knowing me. Instead, I stuck the envelope out in front of me.

"Thanks, Foster," I murmured.

"Of course, Piper," he responded.

"I guess my hour's up?"

"It is."

"See you soon."

"Until we meet again."

I didn't want to, but I left Foster and willed my feet to move back to where I had entered the building. Stepping back outside, I placed my hand over my eyes for a moment in order to readjust to the light.

When I put my hand down, Lucian was at my side.

"Did you find what you came here to discover?"

"Sort of." The information, though unlike anything I had ever witnessed before, was exactly what I wondered about. Part of me was honored to have the time to go back and see myself from a perspective unlike any other. The other part was horrified, sickened, and feeling nauseous. Reality was setting in. It was harsh and unrelenting. However, there was one burning question.

"What do you mean, *sort of*?" Lucian wondered.

"I didn't see you taking my soul. The first scene was—"

"I don't know the semantics of Underworld voyeurism."

"So you have no idea why—?"

"I just said I didn't."

I didn't know, for certain, if he was lying to me or not. But Lucian hadn't yet lied. If he didn't want to answer a question, he would say so. Otherwise, he maintained truthfulness. Even for a demon. There was a spark of curiosity in his eyes. He had never been privy to such information.

"Maybe." I mulled over a hypothesis. "Maybe soul-ejecting is never shown. It's a lot to handle, you know, even for dead people."

"Perhaps."

"Because demons can be recorded. I saw when you came in at the end, and—"

"This information is not supposed to be shared, you realize."

"I don't mind telling you."

Lucian paused; I sensed that he was allowing himself to get lost in thought. Though his visage was not what I would call vacant, he did appear further away.

"Why?"

"Because, I don't know. You've told me so much. At my nagging insistence, sure; but, still, you never had to tell me anything. I feel, you know, honored."

His anger vanished.

"Let's go." Lucian nodded. "Our time here is through, for now."

"Okay." I surrendered.

18

Visceral Tale

M Y DEMONIC GUIDE AND I walked the same path we took to get there, except backwards. Lucian's eyes were fixated up ahead in front of him, and mine were glued to him. The thought of living under his jurisdiction, and especially his brothers', frightened me. Though I could handle pain, I knew how day in, and day out, of harsh physical and mental abuse, would leave me a shell of who I once was. Or it would change me entirely.

I thought of Dippy and how we had a heart-to-heart when he first got home.

DIPPY AND I HAD been in the living room. Our parents had taken Abigail to see Grandma Flannery, so they could break the news to her about her grandson's return, and how he had been injured overseas. Dippy'd been resting his head on my lap, and I was running my fingers over the stubble from his jarhead shave. I hadn't liked the way it felt. It reminded me of the day he'd left.

"Dip?"

"Yeah?"

"Tell me about it."

My brother's gaunt face, caved in cheeks, and punched-out black eyes had been an indication. Not as much as his missing limb. Dippy'd swatted my hand away so he could scratch his head, though he moved my cool hand to his warm forehead. He'd let his eyes close. Soldiers did not generally discuss the war. It conjured up too many horrible thoughts and images, but I'd figured he was going to be thinking of them, anyway, so why not unburden?

"Well," he'd finally said after a few minutes of silence. "It was Hell."

"Come on. You can conjure up a more visceral tale for your little sister."

Dippy'd kept his eyes closed, so I closed mine, too.

"A visceral tale." His brows darted up. "You haven't been there, so it's hard to convey it all properly. I can tell you about the screams. The cries, the wails, the guns. Round after round after round of ammo; boom-boom-boom-boom-boom, like this never-ending loop, with the background noise being those cries. But, worse still, was the dead, dead silence. Because we didn't know if we were going to be taking what we had just given."

I'd opened an eye and saw Dippy shudder.

"The smell," he continued, "is death. Bloody death. Rotting pumpkin smell, only with blood. Spoiled, rancid meat. Smoke. And sand. Sand all over. In our eyes. Mouths. Down our throats. We were always coughing; coughing more, and more. Wherever we stepped, we saw carnage. Mangled, burned skeletons. Bugs and predators picking at human remains, only the remnants didn't look so human all the time."

"Horrible." I gagged.

"Pipe, sometimes war is necessary. You know, like World War Two and all. Hitler had to be stopped."

"Yeah."

"But who needed to be stopped with this war?"

"Us?"

"Yeah," he'd answered. "Us."

I had opened my eyes again and glanced around the living room. I'd known if I glimpsed my older brother, I'd start to cry. I'd focused on the hideous painting my mom did several years ago, when she thought she could be an artist. It was of a Geisha. She had a gargantuan fan in her hand, and was peering down at the ground. Behind her was a botched cherry blossom. It took up almost half of the wall, and no one liked it, but no one said anything about it, because Mom worked on it during the peak of her mid-life crisis. I personally thought it should have been taken down, because it reminded her of the breakdown she suffered, and the subsequent detachment to the family. But, it remained, making us feel alienated when we glimpsed it.

"Christ, I hate that painting," I'd grumbled.

"Me too," Dippy replied.

"I don't think I hate anything more than the fucking Geisha."

"That's a little harsh, Pipe."

"No," I had firmly stated. "No. Mom lost her mind during her whole artist phase. And that's when I had to step up and take on the role of Second Mom." It had been the first time I had ever stated my true feelings. But, more importantly, it was the first time I had ever believed it.

Dippy'd opened his eyes, wide, and I saw his cheeks flush. "I never realized that."

"You're a guy," I'd teased. I had longed for a change of topic.

"Well, yeah," he'd said. "But I mean, wow. It's true. You weren't even eighteen yet."

"I know."

"Abby was... what, a year old?"

"Yeah."

"And you were the one who would feed her and change her diapers. You bathed her. And Mom was–"

"Painting."

My mother was manic. Everything in life that was supposed to be important to her suddenly hadn't been. She'd taken the car out in the morning, and returned in the afternoon, with armfuls of shopping bags. But they hadn't contained groceries or necessities for the house. They'd been filled with art supplies. The gigantic canvas and paints had been purchased at some giant art supply place, a two-hour drive from where we lived. I didn't know how our ancient Chevy had gone back and forth each day, but it did. For a few months, at least.

At the time, I'd been a senior in high school. Dippy had been taking a few college courses. He'd needed his thirty credits so he could apply to be a firefighter, which was what he always dreamed of doing. One of New York's Bravest. I had once caught him flexing in front of his mirror, all oiled up and ridiculous. When I'd asked what he was doing, he simply replied "FDNY calendar prep." He hadn't even been accepted into probie school yet.

We'd sat in comfortable silence for half a minute, listening only to the sound of each other's breathing patterns. I'd noticed how I breathed a lot faster than Dippy, whereas he took long, deep breaths ending in slow exhales. For the life of me, I hadn't been able to tell if it was natural, or because of the drugs. His face scared me. It was just skin pulled over a skull. He had bruised skin, the way you'd think of fruit that sat too long in the crisper, and began to wilt, appeared. He'd had under-eye circles the color of plums; chapped lips, redder than a ripe-for-the-picking apple, from his habit of constantly biting until he drew blood.

"Pipe?"

"Yeah?"

"I was so scared."

My breath hitched in my throat. Dippy had never been scared of anything. Not the dark, snakes, spiders, clowns. Nothing. He'd watched horror movies and laughed at them. But even all of those elements combined did not make up one-sixteenth of a sliver of what war horror was like.

"What scared you the most?"

"The thought of me coming home to you guys in a coffin, with the flag draped over it. You know? But not me being dead. Just me being delivered, dead. In my, you know, imagination, I could see Dad trying to hide the tears. And Mom clinging to the coffin. And Abby not understanding much of it, but she'd cry, because Mom would cry."

"What about me, Dip?"

"You... um." Dippy had abruptly stopped and closed his mouth.

"Come on," I'd prodded. "Tell me."

"I..."

"Dippy, let it out."

"I thought, maybe, you would've killed yourself."

I couldn't help it, but I'd laughed.

"And that's funny... how?" Dippy'd wondered.

"Oh, I mean, it isn't. But I'm glad you're home and safe and not there anymore."

"I'm still there, Pipe."

It had shut me up. I'll never forget those words. And, with each passing day, I saw how Dippy *was* still there. It was visible in his eyes. In his demeanor. Visible in all he did. The way he tied his shoes, snapped to attention, jumped when the sound of a *bang* was heard on the television.

I had once dropped a pot on the floor, and Dippy'd ducked and covered. He had broken out in a sweat and took giant, panic breaths. All I could've done was apologize, cry, and hold his hand. He'd sat underneath the kitchen table for a half hour until he lopped over to the side and curled up in the fetal position. I'd put a pillow under his head, slipped two Clonopin between his lips, and had him sip from a bendy straw.

When his breathing had calmed down, I'd smoothed damp wash cloths over his skin; his face, neck, and shoulders. I had managed to drag him by his arms over to the sofa when the pill took effect. Dippy was a log with two very long arms, easy to drag. It wasn't easy to get him onto the sofa, so I didn't bother. I'd left him on the floor, on the dense carpeting. I had covered him up with my favorite blanket—an old family heirloom Grandma Marino had knitted. It smelled like sunshine and was comprised of interwoven soft, fuzzy string in various shades of yellow.

Back in the living room, Dippy had poked at my nose and woke me from my daze.

"Huh?"

"I asked you a question," he'd laughed.

"What was it?"

"Do you think she regrets it? The neglect, I mean."

"No. I mean, probably not. She never speaks about it. And when I try, she snaps at me. I guess she's embarrassed. But she went through a lot at the time. Grandma's diagnosis. Abby becoming a toddler. Your decision to be a firefighter."

Dippy'd shaken his head. "I should've followed through with probie school."

"Probably, yeah."

"But I didn't."

"No."

"And now my leg is gone."

"Yeah."

"Goddamn campus recruiters."

"Yeah."

Dippy, all young and vibrant and impressionable, had been walking across campus to get from his math class to English. His class had let out early, so he'd wandered into what the school refers to as the "Campus Center" which had been home to the bookstore, radio station, cafeteria, and student organizations for nerds—the college newspapers. Dippy'd told me the story years ago, and it will never leave my mind.

"Hey!" the recruiter had called out. He was tan-skinned and had been wearing a dark beige shirt, covered in medals. His head was shaved, save for a bit on top. Both he and Dippy were the same height.

Dippy'd merely given a nod of his head and continued walking.

There was a job fair going on, but he hadn't been interested. What he'd cared about was getting his next class over with, so he could go home and play video games and bullshit on the phone with Grandma Flannery. It was because of her that he had owned his Confederate Flag t-shirt. And it was because of her that he had hatred and racism inside of him.

The Marine had followed after my brother and smiled. His teeth, Dippy told me, were bright rows of Chicklets.

"Hey, man!" the recruiter'd shouted. He'd been all friendly and upbeat. "I'm David. David Armstrong. You look like someone who might be interested in my line of work."

"What, recruiting?"

"Nah, I mean being a soldier. For the United States Marine Corps."

"Why would I be interested in that?" Dippy'd scoffed.

"Because," David Armstrong had continued, "There are so many benefits. You can get your education paid for. We know how hard it is to pay all of your tuition. And you get to defend this incredible country of ours. As a New Yorker, don't you feel compelled, to, you know, get out there and give it back?"

In fact, Dippy had mulled it over.

September eleventh had broken our hearts. My dad had been down in lower on a job and we never knew if he would make it home. When he had walked through the door, though, he brought a new appreciation of life along with it.

"I guess I've thought about it," Dippy had finally confided.

"What's your name, bro?"

"Dennis. Marino."

"Dennis Marino, there's a whole other world out there, man, waiting for you to explore it. Take this pamphlet."

And he did.

And he signed up.

And our world changed.

I WAS BACK WITH Lucian. My daydream dissipated, shattered into fragments getting smaller, and smaller, until they were completely gone. Non-existent. I was exhausted, and just wanted to sleep. A deep, relaxed sleep, free of dreams.

The kind of sleep where time ceases to matter. Where nothing matters, except having a soft pillow under your head, and a cozy blanket to cuddle up underneath. Twelve full hours of uninterrupted snoozing. It was exactly what I needed.

We were almost back at our starting point, again. I stopped for a moment to give my legs a rest. My guide was a foot taller than I, so taking quick strides wore me out. I know how it displeased him, but he was too uptight to give me a piggy-back ride. Not that I would ask, but the thought alone was enough to make the corner of my mouth twitch.

The sky was pitch black again; inky and wet. I wanted to touch it, to see if it had a texture.

"Hey, Lucian?"

"What?"

"What if this is all just a dream?"

"Are dreams this elaborate?"

"Don't you dream?"

"No."

I bit down on my lip and dropped my hands to my side. It was such a foreign idea to not dream. I knew a few people who claimed how they didn't dream. I, however, was a massive dreamer. My dreams had cinematic production, too. Vivid color and sound. I could see, smell, taste, hear, and touch everything. Sometimes I would fly. I always liked those dreams best.

"I dream all the time," I whispered.

"Congratulations, Piper."

His response caused me to wonder if he was jealous or not.

"Do you even sleep?"

"No."

"Rough."

The demon fascinated me. There were millions of questions just scrolling across the inside of my brain, and I desperately wanted to spew them all out. Lucian wouldn't go for it, though. More and more, he was becoming annoyed. His brothers appeared to have gotten under his skin, but maybe it was just me that worked my way beneath the layers. I was far too new to his world to understand any of it.

He moved his arms around me and tensed up. I closed my eyes, knowing what was coming next. We were whooshed away, moving up and up. The giant tornado surrounded us, and then there was nothingness for a moment.

My ears rang and popped.

I was standing in my bedroom with Lucian, and it was as though the whole world around us hiccupped. Immediately I checked the time. Not one minute had passed.

"Sick," I murmured.

Lucian ignored me, and, instead, flicked his gaze to the balcony.

"Perfect night for a soul ejection."

I raked my hair back with my fingers, and a whine escaped my lips.

"Look," I sighed. "If it's all the same to you, can't we do this tomorrow?"

"No."

"But, I mean, it isn't even raining."

"I can make it rain. And thunder. All the elements you'll need."

Immediately, I thought of how I had once been pulled over by a police officer for speeding.

I threw myself down onto the floor and buried my face in my hands.

"Please, Lucian, give me until tomorrow. Tomorrow night. I have to say my goodbyes first. Real goodbyes this time. And then I'll go with you. Just, please."

"You're embarrassing yourself," Lucian drawled. "You didn't care about real goodbyes the first time."

"But." I sniffled. "I didn't know anything then. I know… I just know things now. Please. Lucian. Please."

He roared with anger; there was a discernible shift in his appearance; I couldn't quite put my finger on it, but, quickly—too quickly—he was normal once more. I curled up and wrapped my arms around my knees, attempting to draw myself in as much as possible.

"You are the biggest—the most—the hardest suicide I've dealt with so far. And that is saying something. Do you know how large my quota is?"

"Just one more day, please?" I begged.

"Why should I?"

He did have a fair question. Why should he? If he were human, I could spew out a whole host of humane reasons. I had I-Love-Yous to share. People to hug. Prayers to say, candles to light, and peace to be achieved within myself. But you couldn't just reason with a demon.

"Well, you're going to be with me for eternity. One more day without me is like the vacation before you have to get back to things. Reality. And I just want to say good-bye. We both win."

Lucian went quiet.

I stood up and rocked back and forth on my feet.

"Okay," he agreed. "I'll be back here tomorrow at the stroke of midnight. You'll be coming with me, which will be the end of it. Why you even want to prolong this is simply beyond me."

I realized how dry my throat was. "Okay," I managed to choke out.

And Lucian was gone.

19

Communion

I SLUMPED DOWN ONTO my bed. The sheets were warm and inviting. When my head hit the pillow, there was nothing but blackness. I wanted the felling all the time: a sense of peace and calmness. Sure, I had slept my life away, but at least it was relaxing.

What woke me were the sounds of birds chirping. I smiled against the blanket. When my eyes fluttered open, they were met by the sun: bright, warm, inviting. I slowly rolled over onto my side, and sat up. It was obvious I was alive, but it was only until I went downstairs that confirmed this was the real deal: my parents were sitting in the kitchen, shuffling through paperwork. They had both decided to take their personal vacations from work after my "accident" became even more serious. I knew they were exploring different psychologists. Ones who specialized in dealing with troubled twenty-somethings.

"G'morning." I wished the terms were different, and knew, despite the odds, I had to make them different. I only had until midnight. It was ridiculous how Lucian would keep it in the bounds of something so outdated and dramatic.

My parents blinked up at me, and went back to their papers.

"Church tonight." Mom sipped her coffee. "Rehearsal for Abby's Communion. And, yes, you have to go."

"All right," I agreed. I figured, why not? It was going to be my last night alive; I might as well spend it with my family, in a church. Somewhere peaceful.

"You're going to be on your best behavior, aren't you?"

"Of course." I nodded. "Unless Janine is there."

"Don't you dare," Mom warned. "I'll take care of the bitch myself."

I grinned brightly; my mother surprised me and, for once, it was the good kind.

"How's the weather gonna be tonight, anyway?" Dad wondered.

"Thunderstorm."

"You saw the news, kiddo?"

"No. I just know."

"What?"

My kid sister bounded into the room and beelined to the brightly-colored cereal box.

"Piper," Abby sang. She poured a giant bowl of rainbow sugar bites. "Is Communion fun?"

What I remember of my Communion Day was how it was sunny, and I got stung by a bee in the park where I was taking pictures. My ankle swelled up and I had to hobble down the aisle in one white patent leather shoe, and one frilly white sock. I refused to wear the veil properly and kept covering my entire head with it.

"Yeah." I nodded. "It's fun."

Afterward, my parents had thrown a party in our basement, back when it was a family den, and not Dippy's place of hibernation. I was icing my ankle, and eating cheese curls because I wanted to destroy my dress in the most subtle way possible. By the end of the night, it was tiger-striped. My mother was just too exhausted to bother. I secured eight-hundred bucks, though. All of it went to my cremation. It would come in handy soon enough.

I WALKED ABBY TO school, but avoided my family for the remainder of the day, not wanting to get in anybody's way. I wasn't seeking martyrdom. Instead, I wrote a new poem.

By seven, we were all showered and dressed in our church best: clean, dark clothes.

When I walked in, a hand clamped down around my forearm.

Arella was standing there, Hael behind her. I wasn't sure what to say, but I jerked my arm back.

My folks didn't notice the vice-grip and, instead, greeted the nurses. Denny remained back a distance, his hand holding onto Abby's.

"Can we talk, Piper?" Arella's eyes flicked in the direction of the crying room.

I excused myself from my family, telling them to just take their seats and I would meet right back up with them.

Arella, Hael, and I walked to the room in silence and slipped inside. When I passed Mrs. Hennessey's picture, I smiled.

"What did you need to talk about?" I wondered.

The two women sat down and Arella patted the seat beside her.

"We know about tonight."

I took a seat. "Nothing can be done. I just want to spend my last few hours with my family. I'm ashamed, and I know I did everything incorrectly, so can I please just go now?"

Arella pursed her lips. "There's never a reason to give up hope."

"No," Hael said. "There isn't."

"Yes," I stressed. "There is. I've exhausted my options. I'm coming to terms with how there are only a few hours left of this. And then it's torture for the rest of eternity. I've seen it. It's real." Nothing would convince me otherwise. I experienced the tour; I saw the line-up of other failures of life. Their torture, their spilled blood, and their grimaces. I could hear the cries; guttural, primitive, and genuine. I could smell the earth, the perfumed air, and, stronger still, the hot, fresh blood bubbling out of cuts and slashes.

"Don't you know anything about your faith?" Arella asked. She yanked me out of my thoughts.

"I mean, yeah," I replied. "I guess. What does that have to do with anything?"

"John, chapter one, verse nine, says: *If we confess our sins, he is faithful and just and will forgive us our sins and purify us from all unrighteousness.*" Hael grinned, clearly pleased with herself.

"Is it part of your job description to memorize the entire Bible?"

"Yes."

"Oh, geez, Hael. I can barely memorize my family's cell numbers. Where were you when I was taking the SATs?"

Hael laughed. "Watching to make sure you didn't pass out."

I couldn't help but grin. "Well, thanks."

"Did you hear what she said?" Arella frowned at us. "You can be saved."

"By confessing? A little too late, don't you think? I've

already been down there. There's no coming back."

Hael moved her hand on top of mine and said, "Honey, you can try."

I brought my hand up to scratch my head. Through the clear pane of sound-proof glass, I watched, mouth agape, as my Mom pulled Jan aside. They were almost nose-to-nose. Mom, more pissed off than usual, was not at all intimidated by Jan's size. I couldn't hear what either of them were saying, though judging from Mom's stance, and Jan's pained façade, I knew who was winning. As soon as Mom's finger got close to Jan's scowl, my former boss winced and took a step back. My dad, standing not too far away, chuckled; his oculars lit up when watching Mom yell at someone who wasn't him. With a small nod, Jan slinked away, her skin glowing redder than her hair.

I LEFT THE TWO women and got on line for the confessional. I was never good at the whole confess-your-sins business. It was mortifying. The first time I had been in the booth, I told the priest how I was trying to bake a strawberry cake and filled the Bundt mold up to the brim, causing a minor explosion. It was, I stressed, an original sin.

There were two people on line ahead of me: a kid no older than ten, and an old woman. I wondered what they could possibly have to confess. Maybe the kid talked back to his parents or didn't do his homework. For sure, he didn't stand on his balcony with a metal baseball bat because he wanted to die. The old woman probably just wanted to have someone listen to her.

Twenty excruciating minutes went by as the senior citizen babbled to the priest. Dippy had wheeled himself over to me to ask what was up. He stated that our folks were smiling and whispering to each other. How Jan Quade was so mortified that, according to an usher, she got into her car and took off. I thought, *score for Mom.*

Abby had joined her classmates, and Dippy was all alone with a hundred parishioners doing their best to not ogle at where his leg used to be.

"People are too polite," he lamented. They were so uncomfortable with trying to make themselves politically correct that they just became more offensive and didn't realize it. He hated to go out because of it.

"Look, Dip." I placed my hand on his shoulder. "I love you, and will stick up for you no matter what, but you have to realize that they don't mean any offense. They genuinely don't know how to react. Society says one thing, our minds say another, and we act, like, awkwardly polite."

"It bothers me," he stated.

"Maybe you shouldn't let dumb things like that bother you," I suggested. "And focus on what's important. If you're, all the time, gonna feel aggravated because of the things other people say, or don't say, you're in heaps of trouble."

"Then what should I get angry at?"

"I don't know. Injustice. Hatred. Pettiness. Arrogance. Definitely not sympathy, especially if the root of it is pity, or compassion, or just trying to do what, essentially, is harmless."

"Did you take psychology this semester or something?"

"Nah. Life lessons one-oh-one."

Dippy messed up my hair. "I should call you 'Professor' instead of 'Private.'"

It wasn't such a terrible idea. After all, I would have been a horrible soldier. I was incapable of following orders; I talked back, and I didn't believe in the cause. Individuality was a prized possession.

When the woman finally stepped out of the confessional, I excused myself from Dippy and went inside. I thought I couldn't handle the nose-to-nose interaction, so I opted for the screened confession.

"Bless me, Father," I recited from memory. "For I have sinned. It has been, uh… a long time—years—since my last confession."

"Piper?"

I'm sorry Piper. We have to let you go. I wish it hadn't come to this.

I cringed. "Monsignor Lucas?"

"How are you, Piper?"

"I've been better, to be honest."

"Please," he urged. "Continue with your confession."

I brought my hands up and moved my fingers through my hair, wondering where to begin. My reputation preceded me, but priests were supposed to listen, no matter what.

"Well," I shrugged. "If I had to confess all the sins I've committed since the last time I was here, we'd be here all night, and I just don't have that kind of time."

Monsignor Lucas went silent for a long moment. Finally, he said, "Tell me what's most important."

"Okay. Let's just say I've gone above-and-beyond the seven deadly sins. I've broken most of the commandments. As a kid, I always thought how 'Thou shall not kill' was the worst of the bunch. Only a cold-blooded monster could take a life. But it's what I did. I took my own." I peeked through the translucent screen, and slumped my head forward, feeling exhausted.

"You took your own?" he repeated in tones of confusion. "But you're here. You're alive. You're talking to me right now."

I hesitated. "It's such a long story, Monsignor. Technically, yeah, I'm alive. But my soul's tarnished. And I don't—I don't have much time left."

There were a few moment of excruciating silence. I tapped my foot nervously. "Monsignor?"

"Are you truly sorry, Piper? Sorry for your transgressions against your faith, your life, and your Lord?"

"Well." I frowned. "Yeah. I mean, yes. Of course. Now that I understand. The consequences of my actions, I mean. But it's too little, too late. Isn't it?" Lucian's visage flashed in the forefront of my mind. My nose was filled with the scent of fresh blood and charred flesh; of smoke, of desperation, and the heavy incense filling Hell's thick, almost-tangible air. I could hear the cracks of whips cutting into flesh; the wet *smack* tearing open new wounds, and licked already-deep gashes. I could see crimson leaking down dirty skin.

"Salvation transcends time," the priest carefully stated.

I was still skeptical. "I'm just sorry," I confessed. "For my blindness. My errors. For the pain I cause and continue to cause and will cause, once—"

"God forgives you," Monsignor said.

"How do you know for sure?" I wondered.

"Because He told me."

"It can't be so easy."

"You're forgiven, Piper. Go in peace."

I remained rooted to the spot. I insisted, no. I said how he didn't understand. My life is in serious jeopardy, I told him. My soul is worse off. I needed divine intervention.

"Say the Lord's Prayer and call me in the morning," is all he told me.

I walked out of the booth feeling dejected. Outside the room, Dippy was waiting for me. I wheeled him over to the pew my parents were sitting on. They weren't speaking to each other and there was a program card between them. I sat at the end of the pew beside Dippy. On the other end of the church, Abigail sat with her friends and didn't have to worry about her intact soul. I wished it would always remain that way.

The rehearsal was a blur but when it came time for the Lord's Prayer, I gripped onto Dippy's hand. On the other side of me, I saw my parents join hands. From behind, a hand clasped my shoulder. It was Arella; and, next to her, was Hael. I let my free hand find my mom's, and my family was connected.

"Our Father," we chanted. "Who art in Heaven…"

Warmth radiated from my fingertips. The electric warmth moved to my hands and up to my arms. Soon, my chest was filled with it. The feeling coursed through the rest of my body until I experienced nothing but a buzzing glow. It was like the first time I smoked pot. For the first time in my life, I left church feeling a sense of peace within myself. It must have been what people talked about all the time. I thought it was a myth, something completely fabricated. Or maybe it was.

When we filed out of church, Monsignor Lucas took my hand and shook it. He said how he would speak to me in the morning. I wasn't sure if I would actually get the opportunity, but I told him how I looked forward to it.

On the ride home, we stopped for ice cream. I had

rocky road in a waffle cone.

When I said my goodnights, I told my family I loved them.

"I love you, too," they all said.

20

Cross Through

THE RAIN CAME AT quarter to twelve. A bolt of lightning shot across the sky, immediately followed by a thunderclap.

My family went to bed. My folks were burdened with household responsibilities in the morning, my kid sister had to go to school, and Denny was aching with pain.

I watched the rain from inside my bedroom. The flowerbeds were all filling up with water, drowning the roots.

When midnight struck, Lucian was standing out on the balcony, extending his hand.

"Come," he stated. "It's time."

My heart sank right into my stomach: ice hitting ice.

I got up and opened the sliding door, the rain immediately hitting and drenching me, but it just bounced off of Lucian. It was falling sideways.

Déjà vu.

I thought about Jerry. Jerry, my final friend who was lovely, and pure, and who would be spending the rest of eternity in paradise. I loved Jerry, and was glad that he would be rewarded. No one deserved it more than he did. My thoughts shifted to my family. What were they going to think? Probably, they would be angry. Because they would have no idea what the truth was. They were going to discover my body. I hoped they would shield Abigail's eyes from her dead-by-electrocution sister.

The thoughts dissipated when the bronze demon casted his ice-blue eyes on me. The salty stuff welled up in my ducts, again.

"Don't," he sighed. "You knew about this."

I sniffled. "I can't help it."

"Are those your final words?"

"No."

"Because there are no final words with you." His tone was even; not angry, as I expected.

"No." I averted my eyes. "I guess not."

Impatiently, he grabbed my wrist and pulled me toward him.

Lucian screamed and the veins in his neck popped up.

Letting go of me, he gripped at his hand. It was quickly turning black and emitting smoke. I jumped back, and examined my own hand, safe and intact. When I looked back at Lucian, I noticed his hand did not appear as gross as it did just a few moments prior. We both kept our attention on his hand, watching in silence as it repaired itself over the course of a few moments. I didn't know if it was the same for Lucian, but I was fascinated by it. I had never seen anything heal so quickly. When his hand was fully healed, he stared at me with caution, and what appeared to be confusion.

"What did you do? Bathe in Holy Water?"

"No!" I swore. I shook my head and crossed my finger over my heart. Simply, I failed to admit how I was given absolution.

Lucian took a step closer to me, proceeding with caution, and I did the same. We raised our hands at the same time and let them hover just a few inches apart. Slowly, our palms drew closer together. His hand was twice the size of mine, and I noticed how long his fingers were. When our palms finally met, there was a spark.

The last thing I remember was the sound of a freakishly loud crack, an amplified buzzing in my ears, and a flash of the brightest white I had ever seen. I smelled smoke.

They say you can't get struck by lightning more than once. That it's so rare, even getting struck once is about three million to one.

They lied.

We hit the grassy ground.

"Purgatory?" Lucian was perplexed. He lowered his view to the ground, and then back up to the bronze gate. "Hm."

"Hm? What does 'Hm' mean?"

"It means—it means I'm thinking."

"I figured as much," I shrugged. "Did we end up in the wrong place?"

Lucian nodded. I could see his nose flare, and he cocked his head to the side in contemplation. I awkwardly shifted my weight from one leg to the other, as the demon thought about what had gone wrong. It wasn't something for me to investigate, since I would have much preferred to be home, in bed, with no scar, and my soul still Heaven-bound.

Purgatory was exactly the way it had been, before; I could see the difference in the sky. The color, cornflower, had dim glittering lights scattered throughout. The air was pleasant—more Freesia than incense; a familiar and comforting scent. I much preferred Purgatory to Hell, clearly, though I did wonder how magnificent Heaven must be. It made me cry. I would never know the pleasures of Heavens—the sights, sounds, smells, feel, and maybe even taste. A knot of envy formed in my stomach, but I forced my mind to unravel it so it would be released. As the old saying went, I made my bed and I would just have to lie in it.

I could see Death's DMV, or the Database, as it was simply called; I wanted to go there and say hello to Foster, but I knew it was a ridiculous idea that Lucian would reject in a heartbeat. He was determined to bring me to his domain, where he presided. The headstrong demon was tired of delay, delay, delay. He had expressed how I infuriated him, so it was safe to surmise that I was deep under his skin.

"Let's go," he finally muttered, breaking the long silence. Lucian ushered me through Purgatory and toward the Gates of Hell. As we walked, the world around us shifted. The grass became much darker; the earth beneath it went from soft to hard, and there was less greenery. The air's fragrance switched, immediately, from Freesia, to the heavy, perfumed incense. Naturally, the sky faded into a dark inkblot. I wasn't sure if it was the air, or my nerves, but a chill ran through me. My fate was closing in around me, and I wanted to escape more than anything. Instead, I trudged along with Lucian, though he was always steps ahead of me because of his significant height advantage. His long legs took him much farther than my short ones did. Lucian glanced back at me, rolled his eyes, and halted. "Can you at least try to keep up with my pace?"

"You're tall, and I'm short, and you walk fast, and it's hard keeping up."

"We're almost there, anyway." He scooped me up into

his arms, and I wrapped my arms around his shoulders, unsure of what to do.

"So I'm dead?"

"Yes. You're dead. Lightning struck both of us, but, of course, it did no damage to me."

This time, I sobbed. It was my ugly cry.

"Don't," Lucian murmured. He didn't yell, demand, or sneer.

"I ruined their lives," I sniffled. Hot tears spilled down my cheeks. I buried my face in the crook of Lucian's neck; the heat emanating from his body was comforting. He didn't push me away or, worse, drop me on the ground. Though I was terrified, I felt safe with him.

Lucian moved his neck a bit to make me more comfortable. "Yes, you did. But, worse than that, you took something substantial away from yourself. You handed back the precious gift."

"You keep saying about how precious life is," I sniffled. "Why?"

"Because that freedom, the luxury, is something I can, and will, never have."

I moved my head away from his neck, and locked eyes. There was no malice on either side. Our look went far beyond curiosity. It was one of understanding.

"Instead of having a life of your own, you collect lives. Souls."

"Yes."

"I'm sorry, Lucian. I wish you were able to experience life. An excellent one, and not just some awful timeline of misery. But, with looks like yours, I don't think you would have a troubled life at all."

"Looks." He exhaled fire. "Have you not learned anything? What your outward appearance is makes no odds. You've seen Maya; yet, you'll both be in the same position. Humans are not their flesh, but they make such importance of it. Mortals only have themselves to blame. And then they become so exasperated; and, instead of changing paths, they exit. Why waste life? Yours was intricate and interesting. So much density in only twenty-two years. Filled with so many lessons. Different people. Emotions; tears and laughter."

I never thought of my life as intricate—or positive. I figured that no one would ever want to trade lives with me.

"I made you laugh, though," I said. "And you're not human."

"Yes." He nodded. "The only one to do so."

"Hmm."

"What does that mean?" he wondered.

"I'm thinking; you're not actually envious of my life, are you?" I raised my brows.

He shamefully peered down. I had a feeling that he regretted what he had said.

"You know, you're right. It wasn't so horrible at all,

was it? I was loved. I probably had plenty of years left—"

"A projection of sixty-four more years."

"Wow. Wow…" Numbness set in.

"I probably would've had children. Grandchildren. Nieces and nephews."

"Yes."

"A job I loved. A house, maybe. A motorcycle. The vacation to New Zealand."

"All of it."

I once again found solace in the crook of Lucian's neck. He continued walking, leaving me to purge my tears. When we arrived at the gate, I felt something strange: magnetism. Only it was reverse, and I was pulled away instead of drawn in. "What is this?" I wondered aloud, drying my tears on my sleeve. "Lucian, can you feel that?"

"I can. And I don't know what it is." He was having the utmost difficulty moving forward. He extended his leg to take a step, and the invisible force halted him, going as far as him stumbling backward. If the situation weren't so dire, I would have laughed at the physical humor.

"Magnetic field," I murmured.

"Obviously. But what—what's causing it?"

I raised my hands helplessly; Lucian tried again to step forward, to cross the threshold and enter through the black gate, but he was unable to do so. He tried with fierce determination until he was huffing and puffing—me still in his arms. When he realized that he was still carrying me, Lucian set me down on the ground.

"Cross through," he ordered.

I took a step forward. It was like walking against a wind storm, only without the wind. I wavered, lost balance, and fell to the ground. The feeling was surrounding me. I wanted to get as far away from the gate as possible. It didn't ease up in the slightest. Instead, the magnetism became even stronger with each attempt to get into Hell.

"I can't get in," I declared. "It's impossible."

"Of course you can," Lucian countered. "I just have to figure this entire situation out. You—you didn't do anything stupid, like repent and get absolution—did you?"

"I..."

"You—"

"Why didn't you tell me I still had a chance?" I wondered. "Are you that selfish?"

"I shouldn't have let you have the extra time." He grunted. "You discovered the loophole and utilized it. How?"

"My angels." My heart swelled at the thought of Arella and Hael.

"Angels!" a voice called out, laughing. I had heard it before. "Such odd talk in this neck of the woods." It was Balthazar; the blond brother who took a lot of pleasure in torturing Maya. Neither of us were fans of hers. The thought left me feeling icky, as though something was wrong. I shouldn't be able to feel the same way one of these demons did; I was nothing like them, after all. They loved misery and thrived on it. I was miserable, but didn't want to be, anymore.

Balthazar sauntered over to us and scrutinized me; he smiled, baring his sharp teeth. "Well, well, if it isn't our pretty blonde *Ego Interfectum*," he slowly stated. His fingers moved up to curl a lock of my hair around them. He slid his index finger along the length of my cheek, before moving to my neck. As he headed south, for my scar, Lucian grabbed hold of his finger and twisted it, hard.

Balthazar barked in a language that I didn't understand. "What do you think you're doing, *brother*?"

"Keep your appendages to yourself," Lucian hissed. "Or there will be a problem."

Saying something at that point would have been an awful idea. Merely, I took a small step closer to Lucian. Balthazar was much different than his brother. Perhaps, stranger still, was the deadly-quiet Xaphan, with his haunting green eyes and dark features. They were all alluring in their own unique ways, though I was still under the impression that Lucian was, by far, the most attractive—and, daresay, the least crazy. He had shown me moments of kindness; of interest, and perhaps an inkling of sympathy or compassion. For a demon, he had put up with a lot of me. Something told me that I would not have received the same treatment with Balthazar or Xaphan. The thought alone caused me anxiety. I was glad Lucian had been my soul-collector, instead of one of his insane brothers. Something substantial, far beyond appearance, singled Lucian out.

Balthazar smiled, and licked his lips. "Well," he grinned. "What are we waiting for? Perfect day for a human barbeque."

"Go on without us," Lucian ordered. "We'll meet up in a moment."

"No," Balthazar retorted. "We all go. Should I call on Xaphan, too?"

I sent Lucian a stare that said, *he knows.*

"No need to take Xaphan away from his responsibilities. You could learn a little something from our brother," Lucian countered.

"Just giving my other brother a helping hand. After you, Piper," Balthazar grinned.

I took a step forward with extreme difficulty, and was quickly catapulted backward; my back smacked against a tree with a *crack*, and I was being pulled along by an invisible force. My direction was a straight path to Purgatory.

"I knew it!" Balthazar screamed. "Get her back here!"

Lucian, anxious, shifted in just a second's time; his nose elongated and widened. His body crouched, leaving him on all fours. His feet morphed into giant hooves. Lucian's skin became pure bronze. From his head, he sprouted two horns. At first, I failed to notice, how, a yard away, Balthazar had undergone the same transformation. Only he was smaller, and appeared to be crafted from white gold.

The two bulls charged at each other, I saw, as I was being pulled backward. They were moving closer to me, and were doing as much damage as possible to each other. Lucian was winning the battle by a mile; he caught Balthazar in the chest with his sharp, long horns. Half-bull, half-demon, Balthazar staggered backward. I saw two huge, gaping, bloody holes in his chest. My eyes widened, and I clamped my hand over my mouth. It was horrifying. The dark crimson was visible on the tips of Lucian's horns. He once again charged at Balthazar, his hooves crashing down on his brother's head. For his finishing move, Lucian picked Balthazar up, prodding him upright with his horns, and flung him far, over the gate and into Hell. I watched in complete awe as he shifted back into the demon I was so used to. He had a few scratches on him, but that was the extent of his wear-and-tear.

"Why did you do that?" I wondered. I was still being pulled closer to the Database.

Lucian followed. "I sensed... I had to."

"You're gonna be in so much trouble!"

"I don't care. This is as close to alive as I've ever known."

I smiled at my demon. "I'm glad. But, um, I don't know what's going on."

"You were redeemed." He shook his head. "I can't believe it. After everything you've put me through."

"Sorry." I lifted my shoulder apologetically. "As much as I enjoy your company…"

Lucian laughed again. I joined in. He walked alongside of me, and we both stopped when we hit the stairs to the Database. Lucian picked me up and placed me on the top step. He stood a few steps down, making us eye-to-eye. His appearance had changed, though not dramatically. I could see a flicker of a smile, and a softening of his usually-hard features. The laughter had done something to change him. Though, just a moment later, he grimaced and I could see him squint. Arella and Hael, dressed to the nines in their angel gear, were glowing white light. I saw Foster behind them, his immense pools of eyes shining.

"Time to go," Arella smiled.

Lucian and I stared at each other. He performed a gesture I would have never expected: Lucian leaned into me, brushed his lips against mine, and stated, "If the sky were to suddenly open up, there would be no law, there would be no rule. There would only be you and your memories."

I smiled. "What are the chances of that happening?"

Lucian closed his eyes and kissed me; it became nearly impossible to breathe. His kiss was nothing short of electrifying. And, in fact, the sky *did* open up. I kissed him back, allowing myself to get lost in the feeling of our connection. Then I heard a frighteningly loud crack, an amplified buzzing in my ears, and a flash of the brightest white I had ever seen. I smelled smoke.

21

Nirvana

WHEN I OPENED MY eyes, I had to squint so the harshness of the light wouldn't hurt so much. It was like when I would go back inside after spending hours and hours in the snow, only reversed. Instead of seeing dark, I saw light. Lots of it. Somewhere in the distance, I heard soft, slow, rhythmic beeping. Again.

I didn't know where I was; only that Lucian's presence was gone.

"They say you can't get struck by lightning more than once. That it's so rare, even getting struck once is about three million to one," a familiar voice was saying. It was Dippy's.

I moved my hand up to block out some of the brightness. "Where am I?"

"Piper, you're safe. You're in the back of my ambulance," replied the voice of Riley Zanetti.

"Riley? Denny?"

Both Riley and my brother glimpsed me and smiled.

"I woke up, went upstairs to check on you, and you were falling to the ground," Dippy explained. "Screamed for Mom and Dad. Riley was here in two seconds flat. He—" he gestured to Riley, "got you breathing again."

I glanced up at Riley, noticing how his eyes weren't so different from Lucian's. I smiled at him, and he went dark pink in the cheeks.

"Just doing my job," Riley murmured.

"Not bad when kissing girls is part of your job description," Dippy grinned. "For sure, I should've gone that route instead of the military."

"It was only CPR."

"Is that what they're calling it these days?" My brother retorted.

I glanced between the two, my eyebrows rising at the light-hearted ball busting. Both Dippy and Riley had grins plastered on their mugs, though Dippy's appeared more mischievous.

"When I heard it was you over the radio, Pipe," Riley said, "I just flew here."

I laughed. "My hero. Thanks."

"Oh, ah, no problem. Just lucky I was doing my volunteer hours at this exact time. I was only a few blocks away. Well, technically, we were at the pizzeria."

"At least you were saving lives, and not doing deliveries."

"Yeah." He beamed. "I'm thankful you didn't get electrocuted on a weekend. No defibrillators in the pizza car."

We chuckled together; I was alive, thankful, and lucky.

"Where, um, where are Mom and Dad?" I wondered.

"Just outside the ambulance, with Abby," answered Dippy. "They're shaken up. Did you—was this–?"

"Freak occurrence," I stated. "Just a crazy, freak occurrence." I tried sitting up, but both Riley and Dippy were pushing me back to lie down.

"We're going to transport you to the hospital, to get you checked out," said Riley. "Make sure everything is all right. Do you feel—um, anything?"

"I feel a lot of things," I explained. "But they're not shitty things."

Riley laughed nervously. "Euphoria from lightning strikes? Huh."

"I survived," I giggled. "I survived."

I WAS RELEASED FROM the emergency room a few hours later, in the early morning hours. Arella and Hael were absent from the hospital, but I knew that they were with me. My folks and Abby were relieved how I hadn't been trying to off myself all over again. They did say how I should avoid the balcony completely, and I had to agree with them. When I returned home, I crawled under the covers and fell asleep immediately. I had no dreams—or, if I did, I didn't remember any of them. When I woke up, I thought about Lucian. I half-expected him to be sitting on my bed, but he was nowhere to be seen. I thought about our kiss. My fingertips immediately traced my lips, and I smiled. I could still feel the electricity running through them. Quickly, they darted down to my chest. My scar wasn't thick and disgusting, anymore. It was still there, only it was shiny and flat. I could live with it.

I grabbed my finally-fully-charged cell phone on my nightstand. There was a text message from Riley, though I put it on hold for just a few minutes. Instead, I dialed.

"Monsignor Lucas," the voice answered.

"Good morning, Monsignor. It's Piper."

"Piper!" he cheerfully replied. "I'm happy to hear from you. See, I knew you would make it through." The priest sounded jovial, with tones of condescension that said, *you are crazy.* I knew what I had gone through, though, and the monsignor probably didn't believe anything I had told him. Regardless, I did make it. His absolution had worked.

"Thanks for confession last night."

"You're very welcome."

I chewed on my lip and thought about how I had been

fired, unfairly, from Isadore's. Yes, I threw around a frustrated grunt of *Jesus* once in a while. Maybe I had let slip one too many *Oh God*'s, but for sure it was not grounds for dismissal from my job. From my standpoint, Father Lucas and I were square. He had taken away a crucial part of my life, but handed something back that offered me another chance to iron out my wrongs. Shifting blame was a cop out.

"I'm sorry," I sighed. "But I have to let go, Father Lucas. Of St. Isadores. The Church. Catholicism. I wish it hadn't come to this."

There was a prolonged silence.

"What? Piper?"

"Sorry, Father," I repeated. "I sincerely thank you for what you did and, I'll always remember your kindness and help during my crisis. Except none of it has ever been worth the hassle, you know?" I was too young to remember my baptism, but I thought back to the Communion. The bee sting. Mrs. Hennessey's classes, from age seven to thirteen. Being singled out as the "difficult one." And Confirmation, the only time I'd ever known genuine happiness with my religion, and it was only because I wouldn't be forced to go to class, or mass, anymore.

"I don't understand," the priest commented.

"I hear Buddhism is, um, Zen." I took a seat at my desk and opened my laptop, tucking the phone between my shoulder and my ear.

"You want to leave the Catholic Church to be a Buddhist?"

I chewed on my lip and mulled it over for just a moment. It was the obvious choice. I didn't want nothing, but I didn't want more risks than I could possibly afford. "Yeah," I smiled into the phone. I opened up a new document and steadied my hands on the home keys. I typed my name.

"And what do you hope to achieve from this new venture?"

"Nirvana."